Aug 13 2003

Best [illegible]

to Dody [illegible]

Dalton Stephenson

And the Willows Wept

Dalton Stephenson

Baltimore, Maryland

And the Willows Wept

Library of Congress
Cataloging-in-Publication Data
ISBN 1-56167-809-0

Library of Congress Card Catalog Number:
2003093658

Published by

8019 Belair Road, Suite 10
Baltimore, Maryland 21236

Manufactured in the United States of America

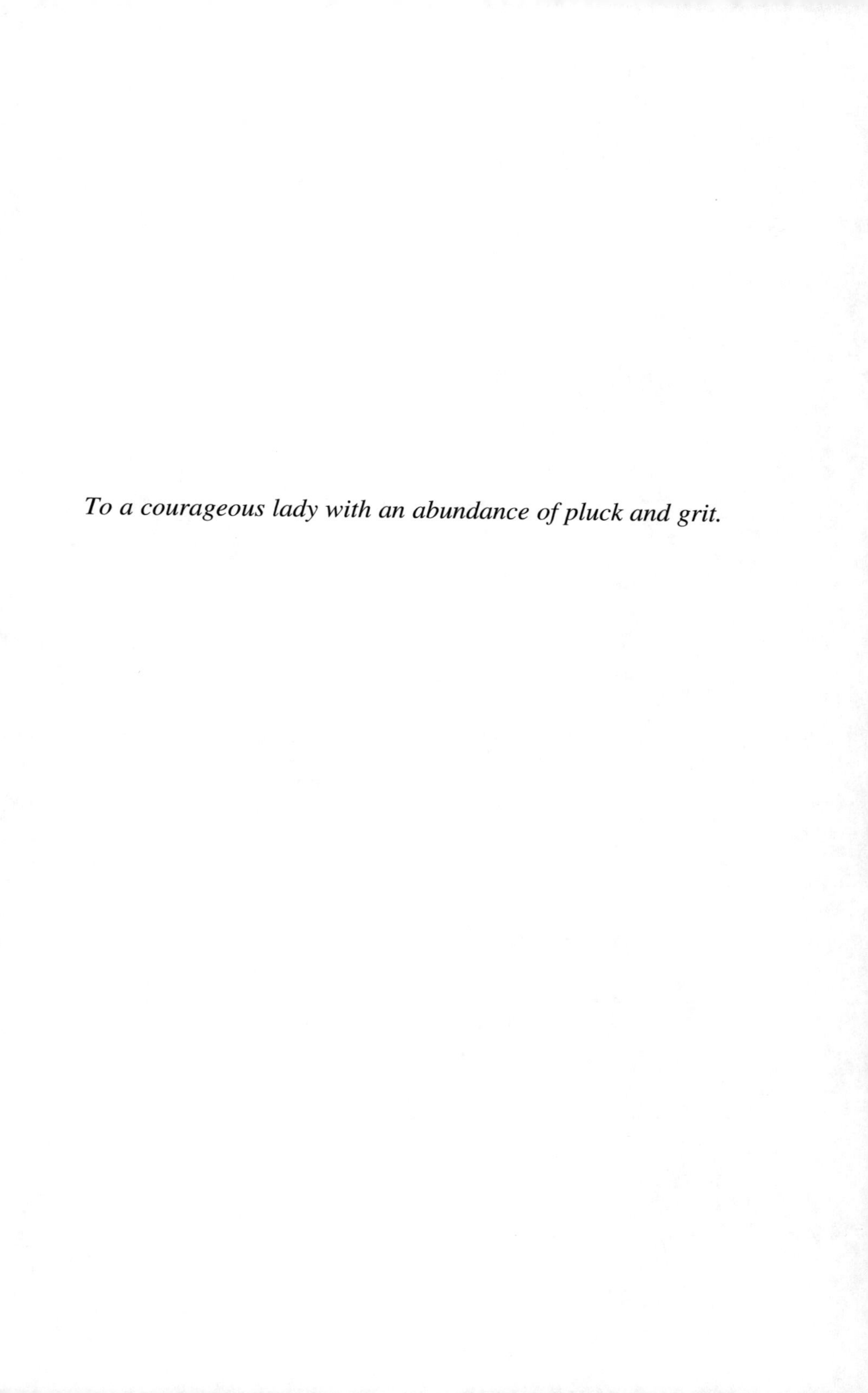

To a courageous lady with an abundance of pluck and grit.

Chapter One

Tennessee Valley stretched east and west paralleling the course of the turbulent river after which it was named. Extending north and south from the main lowlands were smaller valleys, sometimes hemmed in on all sides by green mountains. Atop one of these mountains nestled a simple clapboard house Katie Knight called home. Tourists passing through marveled at the beauty of distant mountains, or valleys that lay between. Katie had little time to enjoy the scenery. Her days began at four-thirty each morning. Bearing a kerosene lantern and a couple of tin buckets, each almost half as tall as she, her first daily chore was getting as much milk as possible from the family's two jersey cows. Hungry mouths were waiting for every drop of it.

Inside the house, her parents and five brothers and sisters anticipated her return. Adele, although only six, was preparing breakfast under her mother's supervision. Infant Norma, not yet fully awake, snuggled close to her mother, who was trying to keep her older children moving on schedule toward catching the seven o'clock bus for the trip to school farther up the mountain.

Later in the morning, Ella's husband, Alfred, would leave for the sawmill where he worked. Often his job took him to locations too distant to return home each evening. On those occasions, he rented a room with a family near his job site and spent weekdays away from home. Presently, he was sawing closer by and was able to be with his family.

With three-year-old Nathan and Norma tugging at her long cotton dress, Ella made her way to the kitchen door and yelled through the crisp, wintry air toward the barn. "Hurry up, Katie! Breakfus' is about ready, and we need the milk!"

"Yes ma'am!" Katie answered dutifully, disguising her discomfort from cold hands and shivering body as best she could. "I'm about done!" Between his wife's hurry-up calls to Katie and the crying of his hungry younger children, Alfred was having difficulty getting his late sleep. His hoarse coughing bothered Ella.

"You kids need to quiet down!" she commanded. "Daddy's got a cole, an' he needs all the res' he can get! He's got a rough day ahaeda him at the sawmill."

"We's sorry," Nathan apologized. "Things'll git better when Katie gits back from the barn!" Although President Roosevelt had instituted programs to help the nation recover from a severe depression, life was still extremely difficult. While sitting at the kitchen table with Norma in her lap, Ella cut slabs of cornbread left from the day before and combined them with leftover breakfast ham for each of her four school-aged children. She then stuffed the food into paper bags for their school lunch. Katie finished milking and hurried to the house, carrying a full pail in each hand, quite a load for a nine-year-old. Drew and Tom had just finished their morning sponge baths.

"Go fetch the lantern before one of the cows knocks it over," Ella ordered Drew. "We don't want a Chicago-type farr here!" While Katie strained the milk into glass jugs through a heavy piece of cloth, Drew retrieved the lantern. Then she warmed her hands briefly over the wood cook-stove before pouring family members glasses of the warm, frothy liquid. Adele held each plate over separate skillets of ham and thick gravy while she apportioned the food items. Then she took a baking pan full of brown biscuits from the oven and placed it on a folded towel in the center of the table. After homemade jelly and butter were passed for each person to help himself, the morning meal preparation was complete. By this time, Alfred had gotten dressed and joined his family at the table.

"We oughta ask a blessin', I guess," he admitted. "Who wants to do it?"

"I will! I will!" Adele volunteered. "Lord, we thank thee fer this food. He'p us all to be real good! Amen." Following this simple, but bubbly blessing, everyone ate in silence, even one-year-old Norma quietly accepting each spoonful of food offered by her mother.

After breakfast was finished, Katie and Adele dipped water from the stove's reservoir, added a block of homemade lye soap, and began washing dishes in their two large dishpans. While this was taking place, Drew and Tom stacked their and their sisters' books neatly, topping each set with the brown paper bag lunches. Katie and Adele took time for their own sponge bath rituals, then joined their brothers in gargling their throats and rinsing their mouths with baking soda water. Each school child had barely finished getting ready when Nathan looked out the kitchen window and announced excitedly, "Cool bus comin'! Cool bus comin'!" With this warning, the family's school children yelled "Bye," as they rushed out the front door to reach the roadside before the vehicle arrived.

"Me go to cool one day!" Nathan stated exuberantly. "When me six!"

"I know," his mother agreed. "An' we'll both be very happy!" Alfred smiled amusedly.

Chapter Two

With Nathan and Norma tucked back into bed for warmth and more sleep, Alfred had some time to talk with Ella before he left for work. "D'you feel awright lately, Ella? You seem to be gainin' some weight." Alfred eyed her suspiciously.

"Don't tease me!" she replied sharply. "As you prob'bly suspeck, my weight gain ain't caused by food. I think you drank too much Hallowe'en booze. I shoulda locked you out that night!"

"I've put you through a lot, Ella. Havin' so many kids in a row has been hard fer you. Maybe they'll come in handy when we git ole an' need their he'p."

"Katie's lotsa he'p awready, an' some day the other girls'll be big enough to do heavier housework. I hadn't oughta complain."

"The boys'll be big enough to raise crops when they're older. The time'll come when we'll have much more income to make life better!"

"My present concern is sleepin' space. So far, we've got by with our oldes' children sharin' a bed, with the girls at the top an' the boys at the bottom, an their feet pointin' toward the middle of the bed. As they git older an' taller, this won' work! We'll hafta separate the boys from the girls. A new baby'll jes make overcrowed problems worse!"

"I'll talk to Paw about this right away," Alfred promised, as he got up to leave. "Oh, I 'preciate the fried eggs you made fer me after the kids lef' fer school."

"I wish we had enough fer the whole fambly, but I hafta save 'em to trade fer groceries when the peddlin' truck comes."

"Things'll git lots better!" Alfred assured his wife, as he donned his jacket and gray felt hat to leave for work. "Fix yerself an' the little'uns some soup fer dinner. That's what our sawmill cook'll be servin' us today."

Ella wondered if her husband would be able to get her father-in-law to rent them a bigger house. Their present home had sheltered them during numerous times of trouble. Drew had had two serious bouts with pneumonia, Katie had almost died from Bright's disease, and Tom's rattlesnake bite just the past year had caused his right hand to swell excessively. The doctor said he was lucky it was a young, immature snake. Right off, she couldn't think of any property being vacant on Sam Knight's extensive lands.

She wondered whether her baby would be a boy or a girl. Had her first son, Thad, not died from a childhood disease in his infancy, she would now have four sons and three daughters, and figure it was time for another girl. Now, with three each, she hoped for another boy.

When her youngsters awoke, she got them interested in some old toys lying around while she mended holes in her older boys' extra overalls. Then she sat down at her foot-operated Singer sewing machine and made her older girls some underwear from white flour sacks that she had saved earlier for the occasion. She was glad the flour and fertilizer companies had the foresight to design their product bags for this purpose. As she served herself and her little ones vegetable soup, she hoped Alfred was enjoying his hot meal at the sawmill. She felt some remorse for her school children having to eat cold cornbread and leftover breakfast ham. "At leas' they have sump'n' to fill their stomachs," she concluded.

By the time she finished her sewing, her children had returned from school. They peeled and divided a couple of large turnips between them to satisfy their appetites until the supper meal. "Take a little time to work on yer school assignments before you start yer evenin' chores." Ella suggested. "Then while Drew an' Tom feed the stock an' bring in wood fer the night from the woodpile, an' Katie does the milkin', me and Adele'll fix supper."

Soon everyone was going separate ways, dong their pre-assigned work. Ella helped Adele peel potatoes and cut up cabbage for supper. In the midst of the activity, Alfred arrived from the sawmill, red-faced from being out in the cold wind, catching nose drippings from his congested head in a big, dark blue handkerchief. "I took off a little early from work an' drove by Paw's house on my way home. When I asked him about a bigger rental house, he said they was all took, but if I'd he'p him fix up the ole, empty schoolhouse buildin', we could move in it."

"How long'll it take to git it ready?"

"He said if some of my brothers'll he'p, maybe we can move in it in a coupla months. Mosta the work'll hafta be done on weekends. He figgered it that way, since ever'body had other things to do durin' the week."

"That oughta work out fine. We can git settled before I git so big I cain't set one foot in fronta the other!"

"I'll drive back up there, then, an' tell him we've decided to take him up on his offer."

As the noisy, two-ton truck headed toward Sam Knight's house, Ella spread the news among her children. "I don't know if I like the idee or not," Tom replied. "Comin' home from school to another schoolhouse might be a little too much!"

Chapter Three

Once arrangements were made, work progressed rapidly on remodeling the vacated school building left empty and undisturbed since Oakdale High School expanded and absorbed all the students from surrounding smaller schools a dozen years earlier. The high school building was enlarged to enable it to house all grades, from one through twelve, in a single structure.

Sam's and Hattie's youngest unmarried children, Jake and Viney, attended Oakdale. They rode one of the two buses that passed by each school day morning. Elementary school children rode the other bus. Bedsides doing housework, the two had to help their mother care for their older single brother, Mink, who was crippled by a severe case of arthritis.

Ella gave her permission for Drew and Katie to take their younger brothers and sisters for a tour of their future home after school one afternoon. The youngsters were quite impressed with what they saw. It was better constructed than their present home, making it more difficult to find small separations between planks or tiny roof openings to let a glint of sunlight in.

"I prob'bly won't wake up to snowflakes on my piller no more," Adele complained. "I'll miss that!"

"But you'll be able to keep warmer," Katie consoled her. "See, Daddy an' our uncles've shined up that ole heater stove an' put new stovepipe in. Maybe we can stay warm without havin' to turn our backs to the heat like we do with our farrplace!" They walked outside.

"I like it 'cause it's closer to the creek," Tom added. "Me an' my brothers an' our frien's can hunt bullfrogs, an' skim tadpoles outta the water."

"An' maybe a water moc'sin now an' then!" Katie reminded him.

"We'll have Drew alone to hannel the snakes." Tom laughed. "One whammy look from him an' they'll scamper to fine a hidin' place!"

Drew was touchy about being ridiculed. Tom's jesting brought him to his younger brother's side in three bounds. Grasping Tom in a headlock, Drew attempted to throw him to the ground and show to all present that the extra strength of his greater age was still something to reckon with.

Instead, with a quick shift of his stocky body, Tom became free and used his muscular dexterity to shove Drew forward. A few steps ahead was a small depression in the ground, still full of muddy water from a recent heavy rain.

Drew landed headfirst in the puddle, making a big splash. A few seconds later he was back on his feet, coughing and gasping for air, his face brown with slime.

Leaving his brothers and sisters in his eagerness to get revenge, he shouted at Tom. "Just wait'll I tell Mother what you done! You won't be able to set down for a whole week when she gits through with you!"

"You've got to stan' behin' me an' tell Mother what really happ'ned." Tom sought the backing of his siblings.

"We will!" Adele supported him. "Drew started the fight!"

Everyone felt there was little hope for Tom. Their mother's recollections of their older brother's desperate attempts to breathe when he was in the grip of pneumonia seemed always present in her mind. Her protective moves on behalf of her oldest living son appeared boundless.

"If you'd pull out yer britches in the back," Adele suggested, "the resta us could stuff 'em fulla straw, so yer switchin' wouldn't hurt so bad."

Accepting the idea, Tom turned his back to his brothers and sisters. While he pulled the backside of his overalls from his body, the others filled them full of broom-straw.

"Whoopee!" Tom shouted jubilantly. "I don't think I'll feel a thing!"

Snickering as they followed Tom's waddling feet, the youngsters retraced their steps toward their house. Ella was waiting, holding Drew's hand as she tried to comfort him. In her other hand was a familiar peachtree branch, still leafless from the blasts of winter. Her bulging figure made her appear more formidable than usual.

"Drew started the fight, Mother!" Katie volunteered. "He put the first lick on Tom!"

"She's tellin' the truth!" Adele agreed. "Ever'thing was peaceful til

Drew grabbed Tom aroun' his head!"

"What happ'ned before that?" their mother asked. "Drew said you teased him about him being able to scare off snakes by lookin' 'em in the eye."

"I thought that was braggin' on him," Tom added, "but he didn't take it that way."

"I b'lieve Drew tole me the truth." Ella shamed his younger siblings. "You always try to take advantage of him because he's so frail! Bend over, Tom."

Obediently, Tom bent over in front of his mother while she flailed him with the switch. The straw worked nicely. He didn't feel any stinging at all! His wailing in pretended pain seemed real to Ella.

"When yer daddy comes in from the sawmill, you'll prob'bly git sump'n from him, too!" she reminded him.

Tom wondered if he could keep the straw unnoticed in the seat of his britches that long. He couldn't recall his father ever whipping him or his brothers and sisters, but he could sure give strong tongue-lashings.

Removing the straw, Tom threw it onto the backyard grass. Then he sneaked into his parents' bedroom and pulled some cotton from his mother's quilting supplies.

"I'll stuff my ears fulla this so his words won't hurt so much." he decided.

Chapter Four

Tom was pleased when his father failed to arrive home before bedtime. Ella was frantic. Not only did she fear for her husband's safety, she also suspected he might not be completely faithful, since her pregnancy hampered her wifely duties.

Katie was the only child still awake when her father's noisy truck broke the stillness of the night, and he staggered in a short time later. Ella, with a kerosene lamp in her hand, met her husband near the front door. Katie shivered.

"What are you doin' comin' home at such a late hour? An' you've been drinkin' agin!"

"We had a rough day at the mill." Alfred answered, bowing his head to avoid looking his wife in the face. "We had trouble gittin' the saw through the las' log."

"It looks like that's not all you had trouble with!" She pulled the small pocket on the upper part of his coat. "What're you doin' with this here ugly contraption?" She removed a condom from the pocket and held it up in front of Alfred. "You never share such a thing with me! I'm not too dumb to know what it's fer!"

"It wouldn't he'p you none in yer shape."

"There was times when it woulda he'ped. You didn't answer my question!"

"Well, it's like this. Sometimes women come on to men! I wouldn't want to be caught unprepared."

"Small chanca that! I think you've been foolin' aroun'. I don't even wanna know her name!" Ella stomped her foot on the floor.

Katie had never seen her mother so angry. She was afraid Ella was going to throw the lamp at her father and set the house on fire. She was relieved when her mother took the lamp back to the kitchen, extinguished it, and returned to bed without saying anything else.

Alfred bumped into furniture as he followed Ella to bed in the darkness. The sudden quietness of the house was frightening in a different way. Katie hoped everything would be all right.

The next morning his family was up and stirring, while Alfred was still in bed. Since it was Saturday, everyone went about assigned chores without the hustle and bustle of school preparations. Katie kept quiet about what she had heard the night before, but the other children were upset when their mother failed to awaken their father for breakfast.

"Why's Daddy not eatin' with us?" Adele asked.

"He's got a headache. I'm lettin' him sleep late," Ella answered, with no additional comment.

"But he still needs to eat!" Drew added, hoping, no doubt, to hear his father tell Tom off for pushing him into the mud puddle.

"We'll leave his breakfus' in the warmin' closet of the stove," Ella replied, loading a plate with food as she spoke. "Why don't you kids go outside an' play a while? You can wash the dishes later."

Katie and Adele thought it strange not to have to wash dishes immediately following a meal. Katie suspected her mother needed to talk to her father some more about happenings the day before. Tom feared she was telling him about his pushing Drew into the mud puddle.

When an hour passed without Tom being approached by his father, he felt better about his chances of escaping further punishment. Drew sensed some of his revenge was slipping away. Katie felt she had guessed right.

Eventually their parents came out the front door. "You kids behave!" Ella admonished. "Yer daddy's gonna show me through our new house."

While their children watched, Alfred and Ella walked up the road toward the old schoolhouse. It was obvious their uncles were already there working. The distant sound of hammers and saws filled the late winter air.

Alfred's and Ella's conversation had shifted completely from the events of the previous day. After greeting the workers, the couple began inspecting the building.

"Can you b'lieve I went to school here once?" Alfred asked.

"I remember it like it was las' week," Ella replied, "even through I was at Grimes School at the time. We was all poor, but I felt like ever'body had more'n me an' my brothers and sisters. We wore our shoes as little as we could to make 'em las' longer."

"At leas' you didn't have overalls fulla patches!"

"I didn't, but my brothers did."

Their gaze fell upon an old desk that had been shoved into a corner. "D'you s'pose yer initials are carved on it?" Ella asked, as she crossed the room for a closer look.

"Could be," Alfred responded. "We didn't always respeck public proppity."

"I think I've foun' yer initials!" Ella exclaimed excitedly. "I'll brush the dust off to see who else's are carved here!"

If Ella expected to find her initials under Alfred's she was disappointed. She suddenly stepped back, flustered. "Look whose initials are below yers - Carol Biddy's! She's nothing but poor, white trash!" She eyed her husband suspiciously.

Alfred didn't know what to say. Carol was still in the neighborhood, and he had seen her more recently than he cared to talk about at the moment.

Chapter Five

Knight family matters ran smoothly for the following two weeks. Ella felt that being quiet about problems with Alfred would resolve themselves more quickly if her and his families were kept unaware of difficulties.

She was happy her husband's brothers were handy to help with the moving. She was getting too clumsy for such hard work, and her children were too young for heavy lifting. They could, however, handle smaller items.

Saturday was a good day to get into the remodeled schoolhouse. Alfred backed his truck up to their front door, and he and his three available brothers began loading, starting with the bedroom furniture. Later loads would take the living room items and, finally, the cookstove and other things in the kitchen.

Ella and the children wrapped dishes, glassware and other breakable things inside quilts and put them in cardboard boxes for the final load. It seemed remarkable that one house was emptied and another filled in so short a time.

The whole family would need to return and clean their vacated house and make it ready for new tenants. Ella hoped they would be good neighbors, whoever they were.

"I hope they have boys aroun' my age," Drew said. "Since my own brothers an' sisters are hard to git alone with, I need some outsiders to share my time!"

Ella felt that older people might make better neighbors. At least there wouldn't be more kids underfoot. She wondered what difference a new baby would make in her own home.

After Drew and Tom tied ropes around their cows' horns and led them to their new pasture, they returned with the older of their siblings to run down chickens and tie their legs securely. Then they carried them, squawking and wings flapping, to their new house.

Luckily, there was an outbuilding suitable for a chicken house near the old schoolhouse building; however, there was no barn. The cows were put in a pasture behind the house. In bad weather, they would have to be driven across the road to the shelter of their grandfather's barn.

Another concern involved getting their vegetable garden planted. Under Ella's direction, her children returned to their vacated chicken house with their toy red wagon and hauled chicken manure for garden fertilizer.

Once gardens had been planted and the weather became warmer, neighbors began inviting families into their homes for an occasional Saturday night dance. When it began, Ella would just as soon have stayed home, considering her bulkiness and her smaller children tugging at her skirt. Alfred loved to dance.

Ella sat in a corner with her kids, while her husband shuffled across the floor with other women. Much to her chagrin, the majority of his dances were with Carol Biddy. While it would have been less disturbing to ignore the bold woman, she wanted Alfred to be aware that her eyes were fixed on them. She felt her gaze might, somehow, keep Alfred more in line.

When Ella decided her husband was dancing too close to Carol, she sent Adele to give him a message. Tugging at her father's coat, Adele shouted in her shrill voice, above the sounds of pulsating string music and cavorting feet, "Mother says the kids're gittin' sleepy and we need to git home!"

Casting an annoying look at Adele, Alfred released his dance partner and went to join his family.

"Do we hafta go home this early, Ella? It's only eight o'clock! I was jes' startin' to enjoy myself!"

"So I noticed!" Ella agreed. "But we hafta think about the kids. They git sleepy quicker'n grownups. An' we still hafta spen' some time walkin' to our house."

"Maybe I oughta leave you an' the kids home nex' time. You would all be more comfor'ble!" Alfred grumbled as they left.

"You prob'bly mean you'd be more comfor'ble. I couldn't keep from noticin' how much fun you was havin'!"

"I admit I enjoy dancin'. It's too bad you didn't feel like bein' my partner."

"I don't know when I've ever been in shape to dance with you, or when I'll ever be able to!" Ella felt that something was abnormal with her present pregnancy. It seemed the baby should be more active than it was. Maybe it was going to be a girl after all!

The children sensed the tension between their parents. The older ones suspected Carol Biddy was the cause of it. They often heard older boys mention her availability. Even their Uncle Calvin, still unmarried and living alone at twenty-five, sometimes spoke of her as the community's live wire.

"Why don'tcha dance with me sometime, Daddy?" Katie asked. "I can keep real good time with my feet."

His daughter's suggestion surprised Alfred. He struggled for an appropriate answer. "The dance floor's not a good place for a little girl. You'll unnerstan' better when you git older."

Adele was bothered by her father's answer to Katie. "Carol Biddy don't seem to think the dance floor's a bad place! Does she know better?"

Ella thought the time was right for her to make a statement. "Carol Biddy knows a lotta things're wrong, but she does 'em jes' the same!"

Alfred cleared his throat and increased his pace as they approached their front yard.

Chapter Six

Alfred's sister, Minnie, and her husband and daughter visited one Saturday after the family was completely settled. Shad Lumpkin was such a neat and proper man that Alfred felt ill-at-ease in his presence. And he considered their only child, Lena, a spoiled brat. She had more nice clothes than his children would probably ever have. He would have slipped out the back door when he saw them walking up the road, but Ella blocked his way.

"They're more kin to you than to me, Alfred! So don't expeck me to entertain 'em alone. Besides, you might learn some good manners from your brother-in-law!" Ella was adamant and unyielding.

"Awright! I'll stay. But I don't want anything he has to offer!"

Once the visitors were inside, and the children had gone out in the yard to play, Alfred and Ella learned the real purpose of the visit.

Shad began the conversation. "On the way up, Minnie and I were talking about how much we could use you at church. I told Pastor Russell I'd talk to you about coming with your kids. Since you've moved, it's so close and convenient! You know our community leaders figured putting the school and the church across the road from one another made good sense. Now you can benefit from that plan too. Nearly everybody on this side of the mountain goes there!"

"An there's work fer all!" Minnie pitched in. "As you know, it's called a union church 'cause several diff'rent denomernations meet there. Jes' look at what they've got me doin'! Even though I'm Church of Christ and wouldn't think of singin' with a instrument in the valley church where we usta go, they've got me playin' the piano fer 'em!"

"I'm surprised at you, Minnie." Alfred appeared shocked. "Maw an' Paw always said it was sinful to make a joyful noise to the Lord other'n with yer mouth!"

"That's talking about inside a Church of Christ building! Use whatever you want to in other places!" Shad corrected.

"I don't see how I can go." Ella answered. "My two littlest ones'd worry me to death with their frettin'."

"How about the resta the fambly?" Minnie asked. "Surely you can come out with the children a time or two, Alfred. If it's too much fer you, you can stop comin'!"

"Will you promise not to try to save me right off?" Alfred bargained. "I could give it a try, I guess."

"I'll tell the preacher to hold off on you. See y'all tomorrow!" Shad smiled confidently.

Minnie called Lena in from play, and the three of them returned home.

Ella considered her decision a proper one. With her new baby due in three months, life was hectic. She needed a little rest from having the older children around. The three hours they would be at church might help her nerves, especially if she could get the two little ones to sleep during that time.

"What can I wear to church?" Katie asked her mother.

"Why not put on the calico dress yer Aunt Minnie made fer you las' fall? It's too fancy fer school, and you ain't been to any uppity places to use it. There ain't even been a funeral to go since she made it!"

"I'm glada that." Adele added. "Funerals ain't no fun! What can I wear?"

"You're in good shape, honey." her mother assured her. "After Minnie made Katie's dress, she set down at her sewin' machine one day while you was at school an' made you a cotton polka dot dress. I put 'em away fer a special occasion. It looks like this is it! There's no need to let 'em keep on collectin' dust."

Drew looked up from his seat on the floor, where he and Tom were putting a jigsaw puzzle together. "I heard some guys at school talkin' about a funny funeral. They said the poor man had rheumatism so bad they had to wire him down. In the middle of the service, the wire broke an' the corpse set up. They said it was funny, but scary too!"

"Did they say what happ'ned nex'?" Katie asked, intensely interested. "Did they finish the funeral?"

"Not til the preacher follered ever'body out to the churchyard, quieted 'em down, and 'splained ever'thing."

"I don't think I'd've gone back in!" Tom commented. "I b'lieve I'd've been leadin' the pack goin' the other way!"

"That's enough of that kinda talk!" Ella clapped her hands to restore order and return to the problem at hand. "You boys need to decide what you're gonna wear."

"My overalls that don't have patches are good enough fer me!" Drew said. "Tom has some patchless britches too!"

"Patches cover up jes' as well." Tom replied. "If the preacher don't like what I'm wearin', he can sen' me home. That'd suit me awright!"

"This is a new sperience, and we don't wantcha to look underdressed, Tom. You'll both wear yer overalls that don't have patches!"

"Will you go with us later, Mother?" Adele asked.

"Maybe," Ella answered. "I don't feel like goin' right now, but we'll see how I feel after the new baby comes."

Ella was reluctant to explain other reasons for not attending church. After seeing that the rest of the family had proper clothes to wear, she realized that her own clothing was too tattered and faded to wear. Besides, she didn't want to face other women looking at her husband and admiring him!

Chapter Seven

Sunday dawned clear and bright. Somewhat reluctantly, the Knight children went about their usual daily chores. Their feelings about attending church for the first time were mixed. While they would welcome extra association with school friends, the restrictions on talk and physical activity bothered them.

Ella encouraged them to step up their pace. "Keep movin', kids!" she urged them on with hand clappings in her accustomed way.

Then she was aware her husband was making no effort to prepare himself to go to church. "What's wrong with you?" she asked.

"I don't feel too good today. I think I'll stay home with you."

"But I was countin' on you goin' to he'p with the littl'uns!"

"Katie can watch after Nathan an' Norma. She's a big girl."

"She's not that big, Alfred! She's sorta on the scrawny side!"

"But she knows as much about takin' cara kids as you do. She can change diapers'n wipe noses as well as you can."

Ella knew she was losing the argument. Her plans were to have the family leave her at home alone for some time on her own. It would be worse being with Alfred and having no small ones to interfere. She didn't feel like giving in to his personal demands. Her mind was on other things, and the attentions he sought were becoming nuisances at the present stage of her pregnancy.

While her older children finished dressing for church, Ella put diapers and teacakes in a large paper bag, and bathed and clothed Nathan and Norma.

At ten minutes 'til nine, the six youngsters crossed the road and entered the churchyard. Drew and Tom relished being on their own, realizing Katie would be busy with their small brother and sister. Adele felt like a lost child, being in the in-between age she was.

Katie had a final reminder for Drew and Tom. "If y'all don't behave, there'll be plentya people to tell Mother an' Daddy!"

As the children entered the building, all eyes turned toward them. In some were reflected pity for Katie being given so much responsibility at her tender age. Others secretly scolded Alfred for choosing not to attend church and help care for his offspring.

Still others thought of Ella and the prospect of her adding another child to Katie's care, and the possibility of more to be included at some future times.

Across the road, Alfred wasted no time in seeking his wife's attentions. Standing behind her and placing his arms around her expanding waistline, he sought to gain her submission. Instead, she pried his hands loose and faced him defiantly.

"Alfred, I recognize yer needs an' symperthize with you. Fer today, I wish you'd realize my troubles. In a coupla months I'll be a mother agin. This pregnancy has tired me more'n before. Another problem is the baby ain't been near as active as the others. I'm afraid sump'n's wrong, an' I don't wanna do anything to hurt the chile!"

In his usual manner of addressing his own problems, Alfred complained. "But what am I gonna do?"

"Cain't you take a cole sponge bath?"

"That might he'p fer a while, but not fer long!"

Then maybe you oughta go back to bed an' have a nice, pleasant dream, an' let Mother Nature take cara the situation!"

Unhappily, Alfred disappeared into their bedroom, leaving Ella to her thoughts. She wondered if she was being fair to her husband. Other men dealt with rejections and survived. She hoped he would be able to gain more self-control.

Ella wanted to look in on Alfred to see if he was in bed. She decided not to, for fear he might see her and think she was weakening. For once in her life, she was determined to put the welfare of her developing baby first. Too, she felt it important to watch her own health.

If something happened during the birth of her child and she didn't survive, the responsibility put on Katie might be too much for the frail child. She couldn't imagine her husband helping with any household duties.

The creaking of bedsprings got Ella's attention. She stuck her head around the side of the door to investigate. Lying on his back, apparently asleep, Alfred had a big smile on his face. So he had achieved satisfaction without her! A portion of Ella's guilt vanished.

She sat down at the kitchen table with a pan of potatoes and began peeling them. "I'll leisurely an' quietly git dinner ready while ever'thing's still. It'll give me some time to think an' prepare fer what's ahead. I want ever'thing to be in order when the baby comes."

Before long, Ella found herself dozing. She placed her head on folded arms atop the kitchen table and allowed herself the leisure of a short nap.

When she awoke, she discovered that Alfred had moved to the porch swing. The clamor of children across the road reminded her that her meal preparation needed speeding up.

"Well, how was church?" she asked her oldest daughter, as she struggled in with her five siblings.

"Awful!" Katie answered, slumping into a kitchen chair.

"Whadda you mean?" her mother inquired?

"Too many hungry mouths, snotty noses, an' dirty bottoms!"

Chapter Eight

A precedent had been set. Each Sunday the Knight children attended church faithfully, thanks to much prompting from their mother. Women in the congregation helped Katie when difficult problems arose with her brothers and sisters.

Ella found herself alone more on weekends. Alfred began making excuses to take short trips to the country store down the road, or to Bosley for a haircut or to purchase some personal items. His absence presented no real problems; however, it bothered Ella not knowing exactly where he was and what he was doing. Male voices shouting, "Hey, Romeo!" from cars passing in the middle of the night helped fuel her suspicions.

Perhaps in an effort to camouflage his own indiscretions, Alfred began to point an accusing finger at his father. In a conversation with Ella, he was outspoken regarding the way Sam was treating his mother. "As I was passin' by yestiddy, I heard foul, disrespeckful language comin' from the house. He was asccusin' Maw of bein' a lazy, bunglin' heifer! He'd better be careful how he treats her!"

"Alfred, ever'body knows yer maw's good as gole. If she's slowed down, it's 'cause she don't feel up to par. I see her walkin' aroun' the yard sometimes like she cain't hardly put one foot in fronta the other."

"If she's sick, Paw needs to be showin' her more concern, not less! I think I'll look in on 'em later today."

"I hope you won't antagernize yer Paw an' make things worse! He does have a rotten temper, you know."

"How could I forgit? He usta whip us boys with cane poles, even after we'd growed up. Many times, if we'd a mine to do so, we could've turned the tables and beat him up. I wonder why we didn't now, 'specially when we was punished in fronta our frien's fer little or no reason."

"He's been good to our fambly, sharin' his lan' and rental houses with us. We musn't do anything to appear ungrateful!"

"I 'preciate the good things Paw does. It's the bad things that're hard to take!"

"Whatever you do, be careful. An' I hope you'll approach him when his an' our kids ain't aroun'."

"Why not now, while they're all over at Lena's birthday party? I think I'll do it right away!"

Ella watched Alfred as he walked briskly up the road. His gait seemed to accent his determination to confront his father. After he entered the front door, she resumed her household chores. "I hope he stays a while!" Ella was wishful. She was well aware that her husband was also temperamental. "The longer he's there, the more I feel like they're reasonin' things out."

Her answer came suddenly, with little lapse of time. She heard a slamming door, and looked out the front windows as Alfred came running down the road.

Ella walked toward him as fast as her legs could handle her bulky form. She met her husband at the edge of the yard. "What in tarnation's goin' on, Alfred?"

"When I walked in, I foun' Maw sittin' in her rockin' chair cryin' her eyes out. I asked her what was the matter. She said she'd took a fall an' hurt herself. I thought there was more to it'n that, so I walked closer to her to have a better look. I couldn't b'lieve my eyes! She had bruise marks all over her!"

"When I asked her where Paw was, she said he'd gone to the back yard. I looked out the kitchen winder, an' he was standin' by the clothesline with a stick still in his hand. Where's my shotgun? I'm gonna blow the bastard's brains out!"

"I don't know where you put it, Alfred!" Ella lied. Actually, she'd mounted it on two nails in the back of their clothes closet, safely out of reach of their children. For the time being she was especially glad she'd done so. She hoped Alfred wouldn't suspect it being there.

As her husband searched under beds, in corners and behind chairs, Ella held her breath. "He mustn't fine the gun now. We awready have enough troubles without addin' more to 'em!" She felt that Alfred could be reasoned with if he was delayed in doing what his first impressions urged him to do.

"If I don't fine that gun, somebody else has gotta answer to its whereabouts!" In his search, Alfred was turning chairs over, flipping bed mattresses and rearranging furniture. His frustration was getting the best of him. "Maybe I'm gonna hafta do a little beatin' up in my own fambly!"

Ella began to fear for herself and their children. "Me and the kids've had no reason to mess with yer gun, Alfred. Maybe you lent it out to a neighbor."

"I don't remember if I did." Alfred searched his mind.

Ella was pleased with her handling of the situation. She heard the excited clatter of children's voices and realized they came from Drew and Katie and their younger brothers and sisters as they approached, kicking up dust and throwing an occasional dirt ball at each other. They had barely entered the house when Alfred left for an encounter with his father.

Ella huddled with her brood in the kitchen, apprehensive of what might be happening at her father-in-law's house. She tried to appear calm for the children's sake. Within a short time, Alfred returned. On his face was the triumphant smile that follows the completion of a successful mission.

Ella gave him a questioning look, without either making a statement or asking a question. In reply, Alfred held up his right hand and folded his fingers into a fist. Several bruised and battered knuckles were mute evidence that they had encountered a tough object.

Chapter Nine

As word of the father-son confrontation leaked out, Alfred became a hero in the community. Sam Knight was known as a dictatorial man. The fact that he never took his wife with him when he made trips to Bosley or smaller towns in the area caused neighbors to suspect his wife wasn't receiving proper treatment.

It was common knowledge that Hattie Knight almost always wore white, ankle-length socks and tennis shoes. Some wondered if the apron she always wore concealed holes in her faded clothing.

Ella remained quite disturbed, fearful her father-in-law might ask her family to vacate the old schoolhouse building. "Where'd we go if yer paw asks us to move?" she asked her husband.

"There mus' be lotsa other places to be had," Alfred answered.

"Jes' tell me of one in this community! All rental proppity's took!"

"But we don't hafta live on Paw's lan', or another place in this here neighborhood. We can light out fer the valley an' live there fer a change!"

"Alfred, you know as well as me that we've always lived on this mountain. The lan' dries out quicker after a heavy rain, an' it stays damper in dry weather. It's a good place fer growin' vegetables an' it'll be a better location fer our boys to farm when the time comes."

Sam kept his silence following the encounter with Alfred. It would have helped if his father had made any revengeful intentions known, so future habitation of the schoolhouse could be settled. If he planned to ask them to move, they needed to know in order to begin looking for somewhere else to live.

It was Hattie Knight who brought the answer. In an unexpected visit, she spoke of Sam's recent kindness toward her. "He's been like a new man lately. I'm sorry you felt like you had to take up fer me, Son. Things wasn't as bad as they looked. I prob'bly made the matter worse by bein' such a cry-baby. Anyhow, Sam seems to hold no grudge aginst you. Sometimes a body needs to be made to think. Maybe you've he'ped yer paw become more thoughtful."

"I hope so, Maw. But if you ever need me again to set things straight, let me know right off!"

"I will, Alfred," she promised.

As Hattie made her way slowly up the road on her return home, her son and daughter-in-law noticed how she seemed to have aged lately. She appeared more bent over than usual, and her hair seemed a few shades grayer.

Ella was greatly relieved to know they wouldn't be expected to move. She could go ahead with plans for the new baby, and she could supervise the kids in the garden work. It was out of the question for her to do any bending to dig or pull up weeds. Her delivery date was too close.

Although Alfred anticipated the arrival of another child, his nature wasn't to become overly attached to his offspring. Rather, fatherhood was a source of pride to him - a time for celebrating the power to produce. Who could tell? He might yet father a half dozen more!

While the older children finished their school year and Alfred worked regularly to earn enough to pay expenses for the expected addition to the family, Ella marked off the passing days on her kitchen calendar.

"The way I feel lately," she thought to herself, "I'll do well to carry my baby full term! I wonder if it'll come early. What if it's born dead or real deformed?" She tried to dispel these thoughts from her mind, but they kept returning.

She wondered if it was too late to change doctors. Although many of her neighbors thought Dr. Phelps was the greatest, Ella had concerns about his personal habits. Wherever he went, an alcoholic beverage was within easy reach. If it wasn't in his pocket, it was in his briefcase.

Whatever his admirers said, she knew it wasn't carried around for medicinal purposes. Her own husband had occasionally followed him outside, where she had seen them through the window sharing a drink!

Realizing Alfred wouldn't support her in changing doctors, Ella decided to hold her tongue and hope for the best. If a problem involving sobriety arose during delivery, there was always the possibility of summoning the community's very reliable midwife from the other side of the hollow. Della

Phifer boasted of never having lost a baby in all her many years of delivering them.

There had been some scary times, like the occasion of the birth of Claudia Malone's first baby. It was as through an overgrown child was giving birth before her body was mature enough for the ordeal. Della had to be extremely patient to save the mother and baby. Had Della attempted to help Mother Nature, and rush the procedure, the consequences could have been tragic. Other deliveries had taxed her patience, but experience had taught her not to intervene too hurriedly nor too slowly.

Her two youngest children crying for food reminded Ella that she had much more to do than spend her days worrying about the safe arrival of her expected baby. There were meals to prepare, clothes to mend and iron, and often childhood bumps and scratches to soothe.

Although she wasn't able to perform her wifely duties as normal, she knew she had to exert certain efforts to keep her husband from straying too far away. She was determined to keep him out of another woman's grasp, if at all possible!

Chapter Ten

Once school was out, Ella welcomed Katie's help with Nathan and Norma. She also used her oldest daughter to do much of the cooking and washing. With the little ones constantly underfoot, Ella had neglected doing something she felt vital - making herself a delivery quilt. She felt this bedding device would not only give her added comfort, but it would protect the other bed covers from bloodstains.

Ella discovered the best time to work on her special quilt was while her children were outside playing. Then she could concentrate on her padding and stitching operations free from the crying and screaming of the younger ones and the constant questions of her older children.

Although Katie was becoming more adept at performing household tasks, she still needed her mother's help in making decisions that would shield her youthful endeavors from criticism.

The older boys and Adele were curious about the "shrunk quilt" their mother was making. "On a chilly night, it looks like you'll hafta decide whether yer feet git cole or yer shoulders freeze!" Drew commented.

"Who's really gonna sleep under it?" Tom asked. "Is it fer the baby?"

"Well, le's jes' say it's a surprise quilt," Ella replied. "Later on, you'll unnerstan'!"

At last, Ella finished her project. Although it was comfortable, with its thick cotton stuffing, it wasn't a thing of beauty. It was cheaply made from scraps of worn-out clothing, quite drab in color. But it should serve its purpose well.

The job wasn't completed any too soon. When labor pains began, Ella alerted her husband to fetch the doctor. She had a premonition that Dr. Phelps should be around for the whole birth procedure.

Alfred returned with the doctor to find Ella lying in bed, screaming in pain as she turned from side to side. The children were huddled in the corner of the room, terrified, not knowing what to do.

As Dr. Phelps lifted the covers to examine Ella, Alfred ushered the children outside, telling them to amuse themselves and let the doctor take care of their mother. "She'll be awright soon!" he promised.

Within a few minutes, Ella's pain-induced screams subsided, and Alfred and Dr. Phelps came out of the bedroom and approached the children.

"The doctor says it's too early fer yer mother to have the baby, so I'm goin' on a little trip with him. We'll be back soon." Alfred advised them, as the two men climbed into the truck.

Katie was anxious about being left alone with her mother and brothers and sisters. What was she to do if the severe pains recommenced? What if the baby came suddenly? She had no experience whatsoever with birthing of animals or human beings. As the oldest female around, she felt responsible for her mother at this critical time.

As she feared, her mother's travails did start again, and they seemed worse than before. "Alfred! Alfred!" she screamed in distress, not aware that her husband was well out of earshot.

"Daddy lef' with Dr. Phelps," Katie answered. "I donno where they went, but they said they'd be back soon."

"Wet a bath cloth an' wash my face!" Ella pleaded. "I'm so hot an' sweaty!"

"Awright, Mother," Katie answered obediently. "Jes' try to keep calm, an' I'll do my bes' to he'p you stay comfor'ble."

Other than bathing Ella's face, Katie was at a loss for what actions to take. "Tell me what I need to do!" she begged.

"Put some water in the kettle an' set it on the stove to boil," Ella ordered. "An' git that ole wore out sheet outta my bedroom closet an' tear it in strips."

Just being busy made Katie feel less nervous. Still, she realized her mother would soon demand more attention than she knew how to give. She hoped her father would return right away with the doctor.

Katie's brief tranquility was interrupted by a blood-curdling scream from her mother. "I feel like the baby's on the way!" Ella wailed. "Are you through tearin' up the sheet, an' is the water hot yet?"

"Y-y-yes, M-M-Mother, the w-w-water's b-b-b-boiling, and the sh-sh-sheets in sh-sh-sh-shreds!" Katie replied, her teeth chattering in fear.

"Come closer and do what I say." Ella commanded her daughter. The other children stuck their heads through the doorway to the bedroom, curious about what was taking place. "The resta you go outside an' play!" Ella ordered.

Katie was relieved to hear the familiar sound of her father's truck. When it stopped outside, and Alfred and the doctor staggered in, both Ella's and her daughter's spirits sagged. The two men were drunk!

"How'ya doon naow, hawney?" Alfred managed to ask, touching his wife on the shoulder.

"Don't you worry your pretty head none." the doctor feigned professional dignity. "We'll get you through this in the shake of a sheep's tail, Miz Knight!"

Without answering, Ella began crying worse than ever. Not only was she still screaming in pain, her wailing now reflected disgust and overwhelming fear.

Chapter Eleven

Ella wanted very much to send Drew to get Della Phifer, but she felt there wasn't enough time. Her water had broken and was saturating her special-made quilt. Dr. Phelps and Alfred were hovering over her, so close that she felt the aroma of the booze they had drunk would help to anesthetize her pains.

If such were her hopes, they were unfounded. The pain was intense and stabbing. Something seemed to be blocking the downward movement of the baby.

When Dr. Phelps pressed down on her abdomen and stroked it toward her thighs, he was devoid of gentleness. It was as though he wanted the ordeal concluded so he could move on.

"Have mercy on me!" Ella pleaded with Alfred and the doctor. "Be patient an' kinder!"

"Dr. Phelps knows what he's doin', Ella. He's had lotsa 'sperence in this bizness." Alfred hiccoughed, and the smell of booze became more pronounced.

"It seems like the baby's caught on your pelvic bone, Miz Knight," the doctor explained. "I'm gonna have to reach in and pull it out."

"Please don't do that, Dr. Knight! Cain'tcha guide the baby away from the blockage?" Ella was now perspiring heavily. She felt as though her veins were puffing out on her neck and face.

"Sorry, Miz Knight. That would just prolong the agony."

"Alfred, don'tcha remember how you he'ped with the others?" Ella looked to her husband for sympathy. "Cain'tcha use some light pressure on my stomach to he'p guide the baby?"

"We've been doin' what was done before, and it's not workin'!" Alfred answered.

"Lord, he'p me!" Ella screamed as the doctor sought a convenient part of the baby to pull.

"I don't see why there's so much trouble. The head is where it should be. Here's the baby's mouth. If I put my fingers between its gums and pull hard, it oughta come right out."

"No! No! No!" Ella pleaded. "Don't let him do that, Alfred!"

"Be still, hawney." her husband sought to quiet her. "He knows what he's doin'."

Although the doctor was competent, Ella knew his drunkenness was dulling his sense of reason. She braced for the impact of what was to come.

With his fingers inside the baby's mouth and his hand pressed against its tiny nose, Dr. Phelps pulled with strong tugs, not bothering to coincide his efforts with Ella's contractions. It seemed to be working. The baby was moving down the birth canal toward the opening. After a final jerk, the baby emerged, but the cracking sound of a breaking bone was clearly audible.

Ella lapsed into semi-consciousness as her husband and Dr. Phelps manipulated and massaged the newborn to get it to breathe.

"Why's its head danglin'?" Alfred asked the doctor. "It don't look right!"

"You can stop saying 'it,' sir. He's a boy! He's probably tired out from the ordeal. I need to get going to see another patient! Can you take over from here? I'll leave some smelling salts for your wife."

"I'll git Maw to come over. My oldes' daughter can he'p clean up."

With the baby resting on Ella's arm, Alfred followed the doctor to his car. "Thank you fer the drink, Doc. I don't b'lieve we coulda done what we've done without it!"

"Don't mention it! Let me know if you need me again. Your wife will soon come around from the smelling salts."

"Tom, go fetch Maw and tell her we need some he'p with your new brother!" Alfred yelled to his son in the backyard.

"Good news!" Tom excitedly notified his siblings. "We've got a new brother!"

While Drew and Nathan celebrated, the girls had other comments. "Oh, drat!" Adele scoffed. "I wanted another sister!"

Katie felt burdened, just thinking of new responsibilities awaiting her.

"A girl would've been nice, but we can settle for a boy, I guess."

"Git goin', Tom!" Alfred shouted. "You kids can talk about the baby later!"

No sooner had Hattie entered the room and seen the condition of the newborn than her whole being sagged. "Son, why didn't you git me sooner? Things ain't proper! Maybe I coulda he'ped!"

"I didn't see any need to bother you, Maw. Dr. Phelps is a good doctor. He knowed what he was doin'."

Through tears of pain and sorrow, Ella turned her head to face her mother-in-law. "I hate to say it, Miz Knight, but Alfred an' the doctor lef' durin' my labor an' got drunk. I wish somebody sober had been here. The baby's not right!"

"I can tell that, Ella! Lemme clean him up fer you."

With the infant wrapped snugly inside a blanket, Hattie took it to the kitchen. Katie had dutifully left the strips from the torn-up sheet and a kettle full of hot water on the stove.

When Hattie screamed, Ella shuddered, while Alfred rushed to see what was wrong.

"His neck's broke and his mouth's bleedin'!" she informed her son as he joined her. "Oh, the poor boy!"

Ella's becoming semi-conscious had spared her the disturbing noise of the small bone breaking as the baby was delivered. Now the impact of the situation hit her hard!

"What're we gonna do? Oh, Lord, what're we gonna do?" she screamed from the news her mother-in-law had just announced.

Alfred went back to his wife's side. "Dr. Phelps didn't say anything about sump'n bein' wrong. Maybe it's not all that bad."

Upon rejoining his mother, Alfred received other disturbing news from her, this time in a whisper. "The roof of this pore chile's mouth is pushed up, too!"

Chapter Twelve

They named the baby Will, in what must have been inspired reasoning. It was evident that much will power would be necessary for the child to survive. His head required constant support to keep his upper spine from being damaged further. In reaching for things, both hands appeared to rebel as they neared the object and jerk back toward his small body. It was an ordeal to keep any food eaten from being regurgitated.

Having to clear soiled bed linens and wash them, along with her mother's blood-stained gown, made Katie's stomach queasy. She didn't realize having a baby was so complicated. "Maybe I won't ever have any!" she decided.

Ella was glad to have her kids home from school to help during the summer months. Will required so much attention that the others' needs were often sacrificed. When the school-aged children were provided new shoes to wear, they were ordered from the Sears and Roebuck catalog. If they didn't fit right, it was too bad. Exchanging them required extra time and postage money, two items in short supply.

When the new school year began, it was difficult for Will's brothers and sisters to leave him after being at his side for two months since his birth. Because Nathan and Norma needed certain attentions themselves, Alfred saw no other way out than to ask his mother to visit every day and do what she could. Hattie wasn't well herself, but she was the kind of person to belittle her own problems when given an opportunity to assist others.

Whether Sam resented his wife's absence, or felt an injustice had been committed, he pressed his son to file a lawsuit against Dr. Phelps. Alfred wanted no part of it. If the case went to court, his own failings would be exposed. He never told his father the reason, but it was obvious to Ella.

Either in an act of repentance or necessity, Alfred did agree to take Will to see a bone specialist in Birmingham. When he and Ella made the trip and returned with the small boy in a back brace, he became the neighborhood's chief subject of conversation.

Dell Phifer, the community midwife, was one of the biggest talkers. "If they'd had me there instead of that stupid doctor, that poor baby wouldn't hafta wear any burdensome gimmicks. He would be hale an' hearty!"

Most of the neighbors, while showing pity for the child, marveled that his demands weren't greater than they were at the present time.

"He's a miracle baby!" some said. "He'll prob'bly have a very special life!"

Ella and Alfred could see little progress in Will. Perhaps it was miraculous that he had survived birth at the hands of a drunken doctor. It was obvious that additional miracles would be necessary to assure he would ever walk and talk.

When Christmas came, and the baby was showered with noise-making toys, his expressions indicated an acute sense of hearing. However, it was very difficult for him to even pick them up, and much more of an effort to shake them to produce sounds. When Will rolled over in his attempts to play with his toys, his siblings were on hand to prop him up again.

Although Katie loved her little brother dearly, Sundays provided a few welcome weekend hours of relief from being his principal caretaker. However, her older brothers and sisters were far from angelic. Squabbles between them at church still had to be broken up, and personal accidents often needed her helping hands.

At home, lack of parental attention caused problems to surface in the habits of Adele and Norman. Hardly a night passed without the sheets of their bed becoming wet. Ella began having the two sleep side by side at the foot of the bed so the others wouldn't be affected by their bed-wetting.

"How can we stop 'em?" Ella asked her husband. "If they keep it up, their frien's'll all leave 'em!"

"Why not hang the wet sheets out on the clothesline so people can see 'em and smell 'em when they pass by?" Alfred suggested. "Maybe that would shame 'em into exercisin' more self-control!"

"That might he'p, but I have other idees of my own."

"What're they?"

"I'm not zackly sure I'll do it. It's a impulse kinda thing. If it happ'ns, you'll know!"

Time elapsed, and hardly a day passed without urine-soaked sheets hanging on Ella's clothesline to dry. Any mention of the soiled and smelly bed linens caused Adele and Norman to hang their heads in shame, but the habits persisted.

"Why don'tcha wash the sheets, Ella?" her mother-in-law asked. "It'd make fer less restlessness at night on the kids' part!"

"I don't have time fer that much washin'! Besides, it'd wear the ole sheets out. I think I'm gonna hafta take other steps, though."

"I hope you won't be too rough on 'em!"

The next morning Ella went into her children's bedroom to awaken them. As usual, she found soaked bed sheets. Without any warning, she washed Adele's face with the wet bed covering, then gave Norman the same treatment.

Crying, sputtering and spitting, the two children ran into the kitchen, rinsed their faces in a pan of water setting on the shelf, and filled their mouths from the bucket of drinking water beside the pan. Then they swished the water between their teeth, and ran to the back porch to expel it.

"How couldja do that to us?" Adele asked her mother. "We can't he'p doin' what we do!"

"Why don'tcha stop?" Alfred asked. "Yer mother's tireda cleanin' up after you!"

"I dream I'm settin' in the outhouse relievin' myself. By the time I wake up, it's too late!" Adele was still crying, eyeing her mother with disgust.

"Me think me's standin' behin' the barn about to go, and when me wakes up, me's already went!" Nathan defended himself.

"I won't do it agin." Ella repented. "But I'll hafta keep remindin' you to try harder to quit till you do."

"We'll do our bes'." Adele promised. "It's not pleasant fer us, either. Jes' don't bathe our faces that way any more!"

"Could I wash the sheets?" Katie volunteered.

"Not yet," her mother replied. "Maybe we'll talk about that later."

Chapter Thirteen

Before catching the bus to school, Jake came down the road to tell his sister-in-law that his mother wouldn't be able to help her that day. "Viney visited Minnie over the weekend an' got caught in a rain shower on the way home. She's coughin' an' wheezin' sump'n awful. Maw said she needs to stay with her an' keep her doctored up."

As Jake left to await the bus, Ella turned to Alfred, who was about to leave for the sawmill. "I'm not up to carryin' on without he'p. As much as I hate to use her, I think you'd better go git Maw. Don't bring Otha, though. I don't wanna listen to her bein' scolded all day long!"

"Okay, but I've gotta leave right away. I'll eat my sausage an' biscuits on the way so I won't be late on the job." So saying, Alfred grabbed a handful of breakfast food and left. He hoped his mother-in-law wouldn't insist on bringing Otha with her. The child couldn't do anything without her mother criticizing her. Nelda never let her go to school anywhere, using "childhood convulsions" for an excuse, although she had long outgrown them before reaching school age.

Nelda Wyatt was a very self-assertive woman. Her great-grandmother was a stern Cherokee Indian, a fact duplicated in her own high cheekbones and dark hair and skin. The difficult life of her ancestors seemed to resurface in her. Her Scotch-Irish husband, Drayton, had been dead for a number of years. She lived meagerly on income from land he had left her, in a simple farmhouse on the other side of the mountain. Her son, Langston, and his wife, Tizzie, shared her home, as did Nelda's single daughter, Otha. Her other five married children lived on nearby farms.

Nelda was agreeable to making the trip, and was willing to leave Otha at home with Tizzie. But she had a request to make of Alfred. "Tell yer fo'ks I don't want anybody crossin' me! It's sump'n I won't stan' fer. I've been aroun' a long time and learnt a lot from livin'. What I say goes!

Ella an' yer kids need to know that. When I'm in yer house lookin' after the baby, it's han's off 'cept for me an' Ella!"

"Be sure you tell the kids before you start pushin' 'em aroun'. They're all crazy about little Will. You'll need to tell 'em the rules yerself. They've awready gone to school."

"It won' take 'em long to learn. I'll see to that!"

When her mother stalked into the room, her tall, skinny frame loomed ominous as a threatening tornado. Ella's recollections of her resurfaced, briefly recounting the numerous times she and her sisters were knocked and pushed around for failing to live up to expectations. Alfred said a quick goodbye and gladly left the women to their chores.

"It's good to see you, Maw." Ella lied, trying to be pleasant. "Glad you was willin' to come over." Nathan and Norma spoke to their grandmother before running outside to play in the front yard.

"'Tain't a case zackly of bein' willin', chile," her mother replied, sitting down in a chair beside her daughter. "What else could I do? Sorry you jes' now realized you needed me!"

"Miz Knight has been he'pin' me. It's so handy fer her. But today Viney's sick an' home from school, so she's with her, doctorin' her up."

"It's jes' as well I'm here, an' I'd jes' as soon git started. Gimme the baby!"

"As you can see, he's wearin' a back brace, but you still need to support his head." Ella reluctantly gave Will to her mother.

"You don't hafta tell me that! Alfred said he was hurt at birth. I can tell by lookin' what he needs!"

"I don't know when he'll ever be able to take care of hisself. If he rolls over when our kids're home, they always he'p him straighten up agin."

"Well, that's mistake number one. You oughta jes' let him be. Sooner or later he'll straighten hisself up!"

"No, he won't! He'd struggle an' cry all day!"

"Then let him struggle an' cry! That will strengthen his lungs an' his muscles. He oughta be ole enough to think about crawlin'!"

Ella could see it was going to be a very difficult day. She stopped talking, asked to hold the baby again, and turned aside to let him nurse.

"How often do you nurse yer baby?"

"Whenever he wants to."

"That's another thing! Too much feedin'll make him fat, and he don't need that. The thinner he is, the better he can move aroun'!"

"But he needs strength!"

"Hol' him by the winder an' let the sunlight hit him. That'll do him more good'n anything!"

Grabbing a cardboard Bruton Snuff fan from a living-room table, the elderly woman went to the front porch. She sat staring across the surrounding fields of corn and cotton, fanning herself and killing flies with a convenient swatter.

Ella was pleased to hear the sound of the school bus with its load of noisy kids. She wondered what her own brood would think of her mother's presence. She didn't have long to wait to know.

"Hello, Maw," each said in their own way, as pleasantly as they dared. "How're you feelin'?" Katie ventured to ask.

"So far, so good!" came the assertive reply. "If you kids'll keep yer han's off the baby, we'll all finish the day in good shape!"

Chapter Fourteen

When Hattie came down with a cold she caught from caring for Viney, Ella's mother continued to help her with Will. Fortunately, Alfred was able to take Nelda home late each afternoon and pick her up before going to work the next morning. Sleeping accommodations for her would have been difficult to arrange. More bothersome would have been her many complaints about the various nighttime noises in various parts of the house.

"I'll be glad when Maw leaves and Gran'ma comes back!" Adele confessed to Katie, as they awaited the school bus. "When I run to pick up Will when we got home yesterday, she follered me an' pushed me down an' skinned by knees!"

"I know," Katie replied. "If we fergit an' go to Will as we usually do, we pay the price! I wish Maw wasn't like that."

Ella learned to tolerate her mother. Sometimes she pretended not to hear Nelda's constant suggestions. At other times she pretended to agree with her when she didn't. The ordeal made her more nervous each day.

As Hattie improved, she noticed the unhappiness in the faces of her grandchildren. As often as she could, she invited them over for cookies or pieces of cake. While Ella kept them reasonably clean, she noticed that rips and tears in their clothing were not being mended, and the garments were becoming threadbare with age. She especially felt sorry for the girls.

As was typical with every family in the community, Hattie traded surplus eggs for merchandise when the peddling truck came by. Without mentioning it to Ella, she took measurements from Katie and Adele, bought several yards of gingham cloth and took it to Minnie to make into dresses for the girls. They were delighted to have new clothes to wear to school.

As usual, Nelda was critical. "What was wrong with what they had,

Ella? Fo'ks can be too proud, you know. I say as long as a garment covers you and pertecks you, then keep wearin' it. What does it matter if it's a little ol'?"

"If Hattie an' Minnie wanna he'p out, I have no complaints. Why should I hurt their feelin's an' refuse their kindness?"

"They oughta know better'n to butt in!"

Hattie's cold seemed to have settled in her back. As the new ailment incapacitated her, despair settled in on Alfred and Ella and their family. School grades plummeted, Nathan and Adele wet their bed more than ever, Will cried for more attention, and Ella's headaches worsened. More tragically, Alfred began drinking more heavily.

These conditions continued for months. Although Nelda's presence was upsetting for the whole family, there seemed no other solution for getting the assistance Ella and Will needed until they were both stronger.

By the end of the school year, Will still couldn't move around on his own. While most babies are crawling before they reach their first birthday, such wasn't the case with him.

"Are you gonna coddle that chile his whole life?" Nelda asked her daughter. "Ignore him fer a while an' make him come to you! Ev'ry time he whimpers, you think you've got to run to him!"

That night, Ella felt she must pour out her heart to Alfred. "She's my mother," she began, "but I've had it with that woman! She's so overbearin' that she thinks her idees are right an' ever'body else's wrong. Now that school's out an' the kids're home, we can manage without her. I'm gonna tell her termorrer that we don't need her any more!"

"Whatever you say, Ella." Alfred was agreeable.

The following day the children kept their distance from their grandmother and Will, and Ella spoke to Nelda as little as possible. In that way, peace was maintained.

When it came time for Alfred to take his mother-in-law home, Ella sat down with her for a moment. "Maw, you've put herself out fer us fer almos' a year now, and we 'preciate it. Now that school's out, the kids can he'p me take cara little Will. We think we can git alone without you - at least we need to try. So Alfred won't be back fer you termorrer mornin'. We b'lieve you'll enjoy bein' with yer own fambly more!"

If Ella thought she could ease her mother out gently, she was wrong! "So this is the end of my efforts! Are yer spoiled kids gonna undo all the things I've tried to do to set things straight? Their hands ain't always clean! Besides, with so many tryin' to do things fer that chile, he'll probably always be a cripple. I'll go if you don't want me aroun', but I feel like I hafta git my two cents' worth in!"

"We'll do the bes' we can, Maw. You know that."

Without looking back, Nelda followed Alfred to the truck with her personal belongings. A they drove off, her eyes were fixed on the road ahead. Not even a glance was afforded those she was leaving.

"Hurray!" little Norma shouted. "Maw's gone! Now we can do what we wanna do!"

"Maw's not easy to live with," Ella agreed, "but she's not all bad. Nobody is."

"Can I touch Will firs'?" Katie asked. "It seems so long since I've hel' him!"

"I'm the oldes'," Drew broke in. "I oughta have the firs' go at him!"

Will was pleased with the renewed commotion around him. A big grin decorated his face.

"Remember what Maw said! You need clean han's when you're aroun' the baby. So all of you go wash with lye soap. Then you can play with Will." Ella was adamant.

Obediently, the children went to the kitchen and lined up in front of the wash basin.

Chapter Fifteen

Hattie's problems persisted. Backaches turned into kidney ailments. Eventually, she was spending a good part of her day in bed. When she ventured outside, she could be seen walking in her front yard with her hands against her lower back to support it.

Viney did most of the housework, including giving her brother Mink the special care he needed. Hattie welcomed visits from her grandchildren, but rarely did she feel like visiting them in their homes.

By the time the winter months arrived, Ella realized she must prepare for yet another child. Secretly she had hoped her childbearing years were over, especially with an infant still not even crawling.

Alfred, as usual, rejoiced at the news that he had successfully fathered another child. At least he had helped get it on its way. The older children immediately began speculating on the gender of their new expected sibling.

"It's jes' gotta be a girl this time!" Katie asserted. "I'm gonna need more on my side if I'm gonna keep the fambly in shape!"

"Wait a minute, Sister!" Adele broke in. "I'm on yer side, too, you know. We both need somebody else to pitch in now an' then!"

Drew and Tom kept silent. They certainly didn't want another brother who wouldn't be able to roam the countryside with them. Rather than risk an additional handicapped brother, they decided they would settle for a sister.

Despite the discomforts of pregnancy, Ella managed to take care of Will without outside assistance. She had regained her strength, and experience had taught her how to deal with her disabled child. Although Nathan had another year to go before he would attend school, both he and Norma were old enough to help watch after Will. Katie and Adele could handle the evening meal responsibilities pretty much on their own.

With Katie reaching her eleventh birthday, Ella realized that she would soon start maturing. It bothered her that boys would probably begin noticing her more. She wondered how Katie would react to them when the time came. She thought about talking to her daughter about what changes she could expect, but decided to wait.

Deep inside, Ella felt her husband was still seeing Carol Biddy on various occasions. She never confronted him about the situation any more. His social drinking had slowed down, and she didn't want to antagonize him into hitting the bottle more heavily. Still, there was something in the man-talk between her husband and his friends that made her sense they regarded him as a romantic rover.

She felt better about her present pregnancy than the previous one. The fetus was lively and there were no apprehensions about something being wrong. In fact she felt better than she had for a long time. Adele and Norman still wet their bed, and Will refused to crawl, but it was easier to take things in stride.

"D'you think you'll need anybody to be with you after our new baby's born?" Alfred asked his wife.

"With our kids getting' older an' wiser, I b'lieve they can take cara things. I sure don't want my mother back!"

"But the baby's not due till September! School'll awready be in session!"

"I've thoughta that. I'll keep Katie out of school if I need to!"

"She gonna need all the learnin' she can git if she becomes a school teacher an' stays home to look after us in our ole age."

"She's a smart girl! What if she loses a week or two? She can make it up!"

"It won't be easy with so much to do aroun' the house."

"Don't worry, Alfred! It'll all work out!"

"Maybe Maw'll git better. I know she'd enjoy he'pin' you out."

"I don't know about her. She looks paler ev'ry time I see her."

The school year passed rapidly. No particular surprises or disappointments occurred to mar the routines of the lives of family members. Christmas brought with it the usual gifts of candy, fruit, and nuts, which the children were glad to get. Anything more expensive was out of the question.

When Easter rolled around, eggs couldn't be spared for hunts, so Ella sent the children into fresh-plowed fields to look for egg-sized small rocks. She then used cake coloring to paint them to be used for substitutes. Other than not being able to eat them, they were adequate fill-ins.

During the summer months, when they could slip way, the older children climbed bluffs or played under a nearby waterfall. When they told their parents about seeing a huge rattlesnake sunning itself on a rock, and how frightened it made them, Ella was glad. She felt they would be around more to help hoe the garden, or prepare fruit and vegetables for canning. She was right! They didn't wander away as much.

School began, and the children were in the middle of classes one day when Alfred came looking for Katie. "What's wrong, Daddy? Is somebody sick?" she asked her father, surprised and shocked to see him.

"I need you to come home with me. Yer mother has a new baby! Della Phifer's with her now."

"Is it a boy or a girl?"

"It's a purty little girl! They're both doin' jes' fine. I need you to stay with 'em an' Norma an' Will so Miz Phifer can leave, an' I can git back to my job."

On the way out, Katie met Adele returning from a restroom visit, and told her about their new sister. "I won't be on the bus with you today," she concluded.

"I'm glad Mother didn't have to put up with Dr. Phelps this time!" Katie thought, as they rode down the bumpy road toward home.

Chapter Sixteen

They named the new baby girl Minnie Vee after considerable family discussion. Some of the children wanted to name the child after Alfred's mother, since she was such a well-liked person. However, no one could imagine hearing her called Hattie.

Adele suggested they name her new sister Midnight, after her grandmother's black cat. "If that sounds too scary, we could nickname her Middie."

Katie thought Middie sounded like some kind of underwear. Drew agreed. "I wouldn't wanna interduce her to my frien's as my sister, Unmentionable."

"Why don't we name her Maude, after one of Paw's mules?" Tom asked. "She a gentle an' nice animal!"

"She's stubborn, too!" his father reminded him. "I've seen Paw threaten to buil' a farr under her to git her goin'."

"I don't think we wanna call her Maude, y'all. It soun's too harsh," Ella decided.

Ignoring all suggestions, they compromised, deciding to name the child after Minnie. Along with Hattie, this kinswoman was among the community's most respected.

Little Minnie Vee was very lively and healthy. From the beginning of her life, she was less trouble than Will, although he was two years older. Her zest for life seemed to inspire him, and he watched her constantly.

She was unable to help him overcome the poor use of his hands. That was a problem associated with his birth injury. However, when Minnie Vee began crawling, Will tried harder to emulate her. His first efforts caused him to do more rolling around. When the two were on the floor together, considerable space was needed for their maneuverings.

"One of the bes' Christmas presents I could git would be to see my boy crawlin' roun'," Ella said, as she tried to position him to keep him from rolling over. But it was not to be. He wasn't yet ready to move around on his hands and knees.

A few more months passed, and Easter dawned clear and bright. After Katie and her older brothers and sisters returned from church, they took Will and Minnie Vee outside and put quilts on the grass for them to play on.

The older children soon left the infants in favor of a game of tag. In their play activity, they knew not to take their eyes off Will and Minnie Vee for an extended period of time. Warm weather meant snakes would begin crawling around. While many of them were not poisonous, there were rattlesnakes in abundance, and they were certainly creatures to avoid.

Not very far from the quilts where Will and Minnie Vee played with their cuddly and noise-making toys was a small log, partially imbedded in the soil. It appeared harmless and far enough away from the little ones to not be a risk of causing injury from falling on or brushing against it. However, there was a small opening under one side of the log, away from the small brother and sister. Inside that cavity, danger lurked.

The slight incline of the ground between the children and the log made it easy for Will to roll over successesfully. In the short length of time he wasn't under surveillance, Will tumbled against the log, and his right hand encircled the top of it. In the process, a small rattlesnake was disturbed enough to head for the opening of its den.

Finding its path blocked by the small child's extended hand, the snake lashed out in defiance. Its poisonous fangs caught the tiny fingers and pumped venom into them.

Stung by the pain of the attack, Will cried out in agony, alerting his brothers and sisters, as well as his parents inside the house. In a moment's time, the child was surrounded by everyone.

A glance at the tell-tale marks on his hand told Ella what had happened. While Alfred overtook the reptile as it attempted to escape into tall grass and weeds, Ella gathered Will in her arms and ran with him toward Hattie's house. "Be sure to tell her the bite was from a rattler!" Alfred yelled to his wife.

As Ella entered her mother-in-law's home, the rest of her family streamed in behind her. Hattie's years of experience in dealing with all kinds of problems made her the likely one to call on in this instance.

"It's a good thing the bite wasn't on his lef' han', closer to his heart!" Hattie expressed relief and thankfulness as she tied a string around the small arm to keep the poison from spreading. Then, using a sharp kitchen knife, she made a small cut across the fang marks and used a suction cup to extract as much poison as possible.

"Now we'll put some snuff on the woun'." No sooner had she said these words then she plucked a small can of the tobacco powder from a nearby shelf and dumped a portion of it onto the affected area. "In case he needs more he'p to fight the poison, I'll tie a pieca fat meat to the backa his han'." No sooner had she said this than she left Ella holding Will while she cut a slab of fat from a piece of ham in the ice box. Then she used a rubber band to attach it to Will's hand over the wound.

"Whadda we do now?" Ella asked.

"Jus' hope an' pray!" Hattie advised. "Before you take him home, maybe I oughta give him a bit more snuff!" So stating, she poured some of the brown powder into the box lid and dumped it onto Will's tongue.

Ella looked at her mother-in-law in amazed shock and pulled her stricken son back. "He needed the extry terbacker to fight poison deeper inside him!" Hattie assured her. "Take him home, loose the bindin' now an' then, an' keep him quiet," she instructed. "I'll look in on him later."

Whether from the snakebite poison, the snuff, or a combination of both, Will turned yellow, sweated and vomited, barely able to move. His right hand tripled in size. This lasted for hours, Ella loosening the tourniquet occasionally to prevent gangrene, and mopping the sweat from his brow. Then the child gradually began getting better, and appeared well on the way to recovery when his grandmother checked him out later in the day.

Chapter Seventeen

After Will's brush with death, Ella was thankful he had been slow to learn to crawl. Otherwise, he could have been on top of the snake when it bit him, with even more serious consequences.

She was glad when school dismissed for the summer and she could find more time for relaxing. Although her older children would be busy helping their grandfather in the fields, Nathan and Norma could watch after the younger ones. Besides, if a special need arose it would be a simple matter to keep the others at home to help.

Katie was becoming a woman, and had to deal with the various problems of maturing. Her parents reminded her constantly that she was too young to set her mind on boys. As she developed small curves to round out her body a bit, she still remained considerably underweight. Her shyness was assurance to her parents that boys wouldn't be a problem for a while.

When blackberries ripened on the vines, Drew and Tom accompanied Katie and Adele on excursions to pick the lush wild fruits. "Remember what happ'ned to Will!" Ella reminded them. "Snakes like blackberries too, an' you might meet up with one out there. Jes' watch aroun' you at all times an' if you hear one rattlin', fine it before you leap, or you might jump right on toppa it!"

The children didn't need to be alerted. Their own earlier encounters, as well as that of Will's, were constantly on their minds.

Tom was a good worker in the blackberry patch, but Drew's mind was full of frivolity. He seemed to feel it his duty to keep his sisters' minds on snakes. To accomplish this, he often slid the stick he was carrying across the ground between their feet. Amidst all the screaming and dancing around, it was a miracle the girls got as many berries picked as they did, or hadn't spilled fruit from their buckets.

"Jus' wait'll we tell Daddy on you!" Adele warned. "He'll heat up the seata yer pants!"

"Who's afraida him?" Drew answered, confident that he was immune from his father's wrath. "I don't b'lieve you'd tattle, anyway!"

"It's not that I jes' wanna see you punished, Drew. You're not doin' yer shara the work an' you're hinderin' the resta us!" Adele continued, somewhat exasperated with her bothersome brother. "Don't do it agin an' I'll be quiet. But one more trick outta you an' I'm tellin'!"

Drew seemed to take her warning seriously for a while, but then his desire to aggravate surfaced again. As the majority finished filling their buckets, he saw a large dead limb lying on the ground nearby. Seizing it and pushing it along the ground between Adele's feet while he shouted, "Watch out!" was too much for her. She screamed, threw her pail in the air, and spilled most of her berries on the ground.

"Now look what you've made me do!" Adele cried out in anger and disgust. "Git yerself down here on the groun' an' he'p me pick 'em up, Drew!"

"I didn't tell you to drop yer bucket!" Drew replied, laughing.

While Tom, being stouter, could have manhandled his older brother, he honored his seniority and joined Katie in helping Adele retrieve the scattered berries.

When they returned home, Ella was pleased with the harvest, except for Drew's half-filled pail. "What happen'd to you, Son? Why didn't you git as many?"

"They pestered me an' complained about ever'thing I done. No matter what went wrong, they all made me feel like it was my fault!" Drew dropped his head in apparent self-pity.

"We'll see what yer daddy has to say about this when he gits home!"

Katie was defensive. "Don't b'lieve him, Mother! He pestered us an' tried to scare us by pushin' dead sticks between our feet. He even caused Adele to spill her blackberries. If me an' Tom hadn't he'ped her pick 'em up, her bucket wouldn't be any fuller'n Drew's!"

"When are ya'll ever gonna stop teamin' up aginst him? All yer life you've acted like yer oldes' brother's lazy and stupid. We'll see what yer daddy has to say when he gits in!"

As the end of the day approached, Katie and Adele braced for what was to happen. In defending themselves, they had received Tom's support. This made him vulnerable to a lashing from their father. Never had Alfred physically punished his daughters, but they had caught the brunt of many of his tongue-lashings.

No sooner had Alfred turned off his truck's engine and entered the house than Ella confronted him with the day's problems.

Following some harsh reprimands to his oldest son and daughters, Alfred's attentions became centered on Tom. "Young man, I've tried to tell you over an' over that it's important that you stick with yer older brother in timesa conflict. An' you repay me by takin' sides with yer sisters agin!"

With these words of warning, their father went to the edge of the woods behind the house to cut a switch. Hardly had he put his knife back into his pocket when he felt a tapping against his boots. Looking down, he discovered a huge rattlesnake seeking a vulnerable spot.

Turning his switch against his attacker, Alfred whacked it across the head in telling blows until it lay dead on the ground. Then he discarded the remains of the tree limb, picked up the dead snake by the tail, and marched back into the house, dragging the reptile behind him.

No further mention of punishing his children for the berry-picking incident was made, as though the snake was an omen in their defense.

Chapter Eighteen

Once Will began crawling, he raced Minnie Vee for objects that appealed to both of them. Most of the time he lost, even when he had a few feet head start. But it was a joy to the family to see him move on his own.

It was necessary to keep pathways ahead of both children clear. Otherwise, breakage, spills, and upsets were bound to happen. In Will's case, once his momentum got him moving forward it was difficult for him to stop. Alfred jokingly spoke of him as a human bowling ball.

During a rare visit, Ella's mother observed Will's unsteady movements as he crawled. "That chile'll always hafta be watched," she surmised. "I think you oughta keep him home an' not sen' him to school when he gits of age. Nobody'll wanna watch after him anyways!"

"We'll see how things look when he's six," Ella replied. "I've awready decided that one way or another he's gonna git as much schoolin' as we can afford. He's got a good mine!"

"With a room fulla rowdy school kids pesterin' him, it'll take lotsa grit to git him edgycated!"

One of the most enjoyable parts of Nelda's trips to visit Ella and her family was the clear, sparkling water they pulled up in a tin bucket from the dug well in their backyard. The opening to the well was two feet above ground level in a stone foundation, capped by a large, flat rock the width of the superstructure. In the middle of this rock, a hole was cut and a round stone just larger than the hole was used to cover the opening to prevent children, animals, or debris from falling in.

The person drawing water was responsible for moving the rock aside and replacing it after each bucket of water was drawn.

Drew had just pulled up a fresh bucket of water and had hung the bucket on a nail on an adjoining post, when Tom called him from the edge of the nearby cotton field. "Drew, come here an' tell me what kinda Indians lived here once!"

"How'm I gonna be able to know that?" Drew asked.

"Well, come look! I've foun' some int'restin' arrowheads here!"

Drew didn't take time to re-cover the well, seeing no need to be that careful, since he had to return right away for the water. Overhearing Tom's excited message, his brothers and sisters followed Drew to his side to inspect the Indian artifacts. They put Will and Minnie Vee down on the grass to play while they surveyed the arrowheads.

As they looked, some of the imaginative minds went back to earlier times when braves hunted the woodlands for wild game. They could picture arrows piercing sunbeams in pursuit of deer and wild turkeys.

They were brought back to reality by Ella's concerned calling through the kitchen window. "Katie, where're Will an' Minnie Vee?"

"They can't be far away, Mother," Katie answered. "We jes' put 'em down!"

"Oh, no!" Drew remembered. "I lef' the well uncovered!"

Spurred on by the excitement in their elder brother's words, half the children ran around the house in one direction, while the rest took the opposite route.

"Here's Minnie Vee chasin' a butterfly!" Adele's welcome news fell on their ears. "But Will's not with her!" Optimism quickly turned sour.

"Quick, ever'body, there's Will climbin' onto the toppa the well!" Tom's announcement sent all the kids at full speed toward the opening in the ground.

It was a race against time. A few seconds separated Will from splashdown and probable drowning.

Breathless with fear, Katie shouted a warning. "Whoever gits there firs', be careful how you grab him. If you reach out too quick, you might push him in the well!"

While they were approaching the child, they realized the super strength of mothers when their offspring are threatened. Bounding out the kitchen door, Ella was at Will's side in five giant strides. She grabbed him by his left foot just before a final surge forward would have propelled him into the well. Everyone marveled how Will had been able to climb atop the flat rock covering the well superstructure.

"Mother, you deserve a medal!" Adele applauded.

"Let this be a lesson to alla you to never ever fergit yer duties!" she replied defiantly.

"It was Drew's fault," Tom reminded her.

"It wouldn't've been if you hadn't called me to look at the arrowheads!" Drew was defensive.

"It still wouldn't've happen'd if the babies hadn't been put down!" Ella continued. "Who done that?"

"Katie was holdin' Will an' I had Minnie Vee," Adele volunteered.

"See. It's all yer faults!" Ella concluded.

"Maybe the little fella shoulda fell in and drownded!" Nelda exclaimed. "It mighta saved him a whole lifetimea heartaches!"

Nathan couldn't understand his grandmother's harsh view. He began crying, looking at her questioningly. "Maw, didja ever fall in a well?"

"No, I never have!" she replied bluntly.

"Then don't wish it on anybody else, no matter who it might be!" In his bewilderment, Nathan ran from the room.

"Aw, shucks, y'all. I didn't mean it!" Nelda flashed a snaggle-toothed grin that quickly vanished when everyone stared back at her.

Chapter Nineteen

With the passing months, Will and Minnie Vee began walking, almost at the same time. It was no problem for the little girl, but it was a different matter with her brother. Just standing up presented a problem. It took many efforts for Will to learn to balance himself on his feet. Then, when he attempted to move forward, he often fell backward instead.

The family was in constant fear Will would further injure his spine or hurt himself otherwise when he fell. Most of the times he got up to try again without a whimper.

Alfred still envisioned the future, when he could rent a farm and have his family make extra money on it. To prepare for that time, he asked his father to let Drew and Tom spend more hours helping him plow. They learned how to space the crop rows and align the plows for cultivation. The girls became more efficient with hoes as they grew older. Even Nathan and Norma learned how to chop cotton to thin the struggling plants.

Ella was pleased that her husband had stopped wandering around as much. He was so fond of his mother that he spent much of his spare time with her. She wasn't one to complain, but her silent suffering didn't go unnoticed in the community. Word got around that Hattie was spending much time in bed. Favors of canned fruits and vegetables, as well as many delicious home-cooked meals, were delivered to her door.

"I wish the neighbors wouldn't be so good to me," she confided to Ella one day. "I don't think I can ever repay 'em!"

"You've repaid 'em awready!" Ella answered. "Or maybe 'twould be better put to say they're just repayin' you fer all the things you've done fer 'em in the pas'!"

"I'd hoped to be able to see Jake an' Viney graduate from high school an' fine good jobs in town. Now I jes' don't know. Viney'll prob'bly set her head on stayin' home to look after me, an' Jake'll more'n likely wanna stay close by, too."

"They've done good to git this near graduatin'. D'you know they'll be the very firs' in the whole Knight clan to have high school diplomers! That's sure be sump'n to be proud of!"

"I'm awready prouda both of 'em!" Hattie corrected her.

As winter wore on, Hattie continued to wear out. It became more and more difficult for her to fight off colds. When a late season's congestion turned into pneumonia, it became apparent that her days were numbered. Malfunctioning kidneys added to her misery. The doctor warned the family that the end was near for her.

Jake and Viney fought back tears each time they were at their mother's bedside. "We're workin' hard to graduate fer you!" Viney assured Hattie.

"We wanna see you settin' in the front rowa the auditorium!" Jake added.

"I can pitcher it in my mine," Hattie replied weakly. "Ev'ry head'll turn as you two march down the aisle with the others to take yer places on the stage. An' I don't b'lieve anybody could be prouder'n me!"

At this point, Jake and Viney could hold back their tears no longer. They hurried from their mother's bedroom to the back porch, where they both wept bitterly. They each knew their mother wouldn't attend their graduation, at least not in the flesh.

Alfred and Minnie also grieved over their mother's fast deteriorating health, as well as did their other brothers. "I donno if I can stan' to live here after she's gone." Alfred confided to Ella. "She's the strong bon' that has hel' our fambly together fer so many years!"

Hattie died a month short of graduation exercises at the high school. Perhaps none were more supportive of the family than the senior class. They came as a group and spent several hours with the family as Hattie's body lay in state in an adjoining room. The community offered support of a different kind. Women from miles around brought in food that covered the tops of the stove, counters and the kitchen table. Men volunteered to help in whatever ways they could.

Once the pallbearers were selected and various others enlisted to assist with the funeral service, several able-bodied men went to the nearby church cemetery to dig the grave. Somber-faced friends removed dirt and piled it beside the excavation, silent in respect for a great soul who had passed on.

At the funeral service, all the pews in the small church filled quickly. Then attendees lined up outside in front of the open double doors, seeing as much as possible of what was transpiring inside.

Flower shop wreaths, as well as homemade bouquets, filled all available space inside the church. The beauty and aroma were very impressive.

When the small choir sang "Precious Memories," it was too much for Hattie's devoted sons and daughters. A wailing cry arose that echoed from the woodlands behind the building. Hand-held cardboard fans fluttered to circulate air to those who were near fainting.

Throughout all the commotion, Sam Knight sat poker-faced. It was difficult to measure the extent of his grief, or the effect his wife's death was having on him. Only time would determine that.

As they laid Hattie to rest in the pretty little Bermuda-grassed cemetery, Will surprised his family with his first grief-stricken words, "Noodbye Nannaw." It was as though he realized the farewell word meant "God be with you!"

Chapter Twenty

Hattie's passing seemed to take away a good portion of the gentleness of spring. Thorns grew thick on rose bushes, and briars became more prolific in fields. Overhead, peaceful skies turned stormy.

Briefly, Alfred took more comfort in the presence of his family. He wandered across his father's farm with his children on his off days from the sawmill, searching for animals or links with his past. At one point, he found a string ball made from sock yarn that his mother had put together for him and his brothers years earlier.

In one of their field trips, an ominous thunderhead arose in the southwest sky. As it moved nearer, its ruffled approach clouds floated menacingly overhead. Alfred stopped and surveyed the thunderstorm as it grew continually more boisterous. The noise of thunder accompanying lightning strikes echoed across the mountainous hills and hollows.

"We may have a tornader in this one!" Alfred warned his children. "Watch with me fer a trailin' cloud that looks like a elephant's snout!"

"Whadda we do if we see one?" Adele asked her father nervously.

"If it heads in our d'rection, we'll jump in the ditch over there."

"What if there's a rattlesnake in the ditch?" Tom asked, somewhat concerned.

"Tell him to move over!" Alfred replied, laughing. Then he decided it wasn't a time for joking. "We don't hafta be concerned about rattlers here. The noise we've been makin' has awready caused 'em to crawl away."

"I see clouds going aroun' in a circle under the other clouds!" Drew yelled excitedly.

"I see 'em!" Nathan joined in. "Now they're growin' a little tail!"

"An' that little tail's gittin' longer'n wider!" Adele's frightened voice relayed her concern.

The little group huddled together as the funnel cloud dropped to the ground and began twisting through the woods a quarter of a mile away. "Is it time to jump in the ditch?" little Norma asked. The wind noise was loud and threatening, intermingled with the sound of breaking trees and limbs.

"Jes' hol' yer groun', kids. The small tornader's movin' away from us!"

Ella was less certain. She ran into the yard, trying to wave them in.

Alfred pointed to the cloud, trying to assure his disturbed wife that the danger was moving away from them. Ella jumped up and down a few times, then reentered the back door of the house.

"What would've happen'd if the storm had hit our house?" Adele asked her father.

"It was a small twister," Alfred replied. "It mighta tore a few shingles off or popped a winder or two out, but it shouldn't've done much damage."

"Jes' the same, I'm glad it went the other way!" Katie remarked.

"We all are!" Alfred agreed.

When they returned to the house, Ella had little to say. It was evident she resented their apparent unconcern for her, Will and Minnie Vee in the face of the threatening storm.

If the trials of spring had any effects on making Sam more humble, it wasn't noticeable. More pronounced in his behavior was his roving eye for women. Realizing no matrimonial bonds were now present to exert any degree of influence on him, Alfred and Ella advised their children to stay clear of the man. "Don't ever be in the house alone with him!" Alfred instructed his daughters.

A few days later, Adele and Norma visited Viney for a treat of strawberries and cream. As they walked out the back door, they noticed their grandfather approaching up the pathway from the spring behind his house.

Remembering their parents' warning about him, they hurriedly walked in the opposite direction. The two girls wanted to avoid any words or actions.

"Come here, sweethearts! I wanna show you sump'n!" Sam yelled to Adele and Norma.

As they continued to distance themselves from their grandfather, he was persistent. "Don't be afraida me! Why should I wanna hurt my own granddaughters?"

Adele stopped and looked back. "What's wrong with seein' what he's talkin' about?" she whispered to her sister. "We can look without gittin' too close."

"I don't think we oughta. I don't know if we can trus' him!" Norma whispered in a concerned low voice.

"Well, I'm gonna see fer myself!" Adele replied, as she moved toward Sam. She stopped a few yards from him.

Reaching into his shirt pocket, Sam produced a condom. "D'you know what this is?" He asked his unsuspecting granddaughter.

Startled and frightened, Adele backed slowly away, then ran as fast as her legs would carry her. Norma had already hurried home to tell her mother what was happening.

As they turned to face Adele, sobbing and shivering as she entered the house, Ella confronted Norma with an accusing question. "Why didja leave yer big sister alone with that man?"

Chapter Twenty-One

Ella didn't tell Alfred about Adele's unpleasant encounter with her grandfather. She didn't want to jeopardize her husband's borderline acceptance of his father. Violence could have easily erupted, resulting in chaos affecting many relatives. Instead, she focused on a different protective scheme.

"Alfred, how would you feel about getting' the kids a dog to keep 'em comp'ny an' look after 'em?"

Her husband wasn't hard to convince. He liked pets, both human and animal. "Minnie's female collie had a litter of pups a coupla months ago. I'll see if she has any lef'."

Alfred's enthusiasm made Ella wonder if she shouldn't have mentioned a dog sooner. The animal could be a constant guard against snakes and other uncouth creatures on the farm. Her husband wasted no time in revving up his noisy truck and heading down the road to visit his sister.

Luck was on his side. Although Minnie had given most of the pups away, she still had one male left, a runt who obviously had been pushed aside by his brothers and sisters at feeding time. Alfred wondered if he should pass on taking the little dog. Although frail, with unhealthy looking hair, the small animal had friendly eyes and a wagging tail. "We can feed him good an' bring him outta this!" Alfred thought. He thanked Minnie and left with the puppy sharing the cab of the truck with him.

Ella, as well as the children, accepted the new arrival immediately. The challenge of nurturing him out of his runthood was met unflinchingly.

"He can have parta my supper milk!" Drew volunteered.

"Mine, too!" Katie echoed, although past health problems had contributed to her looking somewhat like a runt herself.

"I'll share my sausage an' biscuits with him!" Adele added, with resolve.

"An' he can have somma my syrup!" Nathan yelled excitedly.

"I'm afraid dogs don't eat syrup!" Ella advised.

"Why, Mother?" Nathan asked.

"Maybe they know sweets ain't good fer their teeth!"

"Then I'll think of sump'n else to give him!"

"I'm gonna give him lotsa love!" Norma decided.

"I gee him paah oh heah!" Will added in his awkward way of speaking.

"Since the resta you ain't leavin' me much choice," Tom spoke up, "I guess I'll jes' hafta give him lotsa my time!"

"That's very important, son." Alfred congratulated him. "He'll need plentya that, too!"

Tom was elated at having said something that his father agreed with. It was a rare occasion, bringing a big grin to his face.

Now that the children had committed themselves to giving the puppy the care necessary to help him grow stronger, Ella felt it was time to name him.

"Can we call him Puddles?" Norma asked. "That's what he makes all the time!"

"That's too undignified," Katie answered. "How about Tiger?"

"You've sure got a good imagination, Sister!" Drew chided her. "He's right the opp'site from that now."

"Then what about Elfie?" Adele asked.

"That's a bit too much in the other d'rection," Tom said.

"All you look at him close an' think," Alfred suggested. "Try hard to come up with a name that suits him now an' still will fit him when he grows up."

After a few seconds of deep thought, Norma felt she had the perfect idea. "Why don't we call him Shag? Collies are shaggy alla their lives!"

The suggestion was put to a vote, and everyone agreed with it.

With the attention given him from all members of the family, Shag grew and matured rapidly. His fur began to shine, and there was much more vigor in his actions. He was a source of much joy for the children as he romped and played with them as though he was another brother.

When school started, Shag followed the children to the bus, and would have boarded it with them had they not pushed him back. Off and on throughout the days that followed, he occasionally looked down the road, longing for his friends to return. Eventually, he learned to sense the time for their arrival and only searched the road then.

When the days grew cooler, Shag took up hunting and roaming woods, fields, and pasturelands as he looked for things to chase. Occasionally, Ella found a bird or a squirrel or rabbit deposited outside her front door. It seemed the dog wanted to earn his keep, and was making his own contributions to the family's food supply. It took several reprimands from Ella to stop Shag from bringing in an occasional snake. Her chief concern was that there might still be some life remaining n the reptiles when he left them.

Ella salvaged whatever of the animals she could and cooked them for her family. She always made certain that a generous portion was kept back for Shag. He had come a long way, and it was important that he continue to grow and feel his worth as an important member of the family.

Chapter Twenty-Two

Alfred prepared his family for what lay ahead. "We'll be movin' outta this ole schoolhouse nex' spring to do our own farmin'. I've saved up to buy a coupla mules an' farm tools, an' we'll be goin' to the ole Jacobs place in the holler. By workin' together, we oughta do real good."

The family didn't know what to expect. They had always worked for Sam, or neighbors in the vicinity. Visions of prosperity brightened their faces. The months that separated them from that glorious day seemed to pass too slowly.

When moving day came, it was much like the day they moved into the old schoolhouse building. Although Drew and Tom were bigger and able to do heavier work than before, Alfred's brothers were on hand again to make the job easier. They had also promised Shad and Minnie their help in moving them into the schoolhouse building as soon as Alfred's family had left.

Adele and Norma helped Nathan and Katie move the cows and chickens. The mile trek up and down the dusty road until all the animals were resettled was tiring. They hoped the rest of the year would be more pleasant.

The Jacobs' place was quite inviting. There was a nice well of cold, clear water where the new tenants could keep their milk and butter fresh, draw water for the family wash, and use for cold baths. The family who lived there earlier had moved to town, leaving behind a huge black iron pot. This object would be ideal for boiling wash water.

Alfred drove his truck to Bosley and returned with two mules tethered to the sideboards. "Their names're Hank and Spike," he proudly announced, "an' they're all ours! The farm store people will bring the plows an' other things out later."

The mules were aging and very gentle. They would be loyal and obedient to commands. "Boys, when you start plowin', yell 'Gee' when you want the mules to go right, and 'Haw' when you want them to move to the left. They'll mine you right off!"

Drew and Tom were eager to get going. It sounded like fun. They began planning what they would do with their share of the farm's profits. "Maybe I can git some cowboy boots jes' like Gene Autry wears!" Tom exclaimed. "I think I'd settle for a shiny bike!" Drew responded, with stars in his eyes.

The plows and other farm implements soon arrived, very reflective in their shininess.

"Where do we start?" Tom asked Alfred eagerly.

"We'll begin by turnin' the lan'," his father answered. "Yer Uncle Splash will come by termorrer mornin' to he'p you git started while I'm workin' at the sawmill."

The days that followed were much less fun than the children had expected. Drew and Tom were kept out of school day after day until the job was finished.

"Mr. Jacobs says we can add to our acreage by clearin' bushes off the slope behine the barn. Katie, I want you an' Adele to stay outta school. Take axes an' hoes over there an' see how much scrub brush you can chop down. Pile it up as you go, an' we'll burn it later." Alfred's instructions were to the point.

After a couple of days, the youths were wishing they were back in the old schoolhouse. "This ain't much fun at all!" Adele complained. "I've got blisters on both han's!"

"My shoulders an' neck're sore from the joltin' I git ever' time I hit a lick!" Katie added.

"What if you had to plow a tractor all night long?" Tom asked. "Would you like that better?"

"You don't know anything about plowin' a tractor!" Adele reminded him.

"I've looked down at the valley an' watched 'em at night. I can see the lights movin' back and forth whenever I look down there durin' dark."

As Drew and Tom were finishing their assigned groundbreaking chore, and Katie and Adele were burning the brush they had piled up earlier, it seemed everything would be in order for them to return to school the following day. Adele struck a match to set the last brush heap afire, while Katie restacked the pile on the opposite side. Suddenly a rattler, disturbed in his resting place, crawled out hurriedly toward Katie.

Her distressed screams brought Adele to her side. Then both girls backed away, hoes in hand, yelling at the top of their voices, "He'p! He'p! He'p!"

Hearing their cries, Drew stopped his mule, rushed to their side, and killed the snake with one of the hoes. "Why didn't you jes' chop its head off?" he asked Katie.

"I guess I was too surprised an' scared," she answered, a bit embarrassed.

Although Katie and Adele were allowed to return to school the following day, and got assignments for making up lost time, Tom's and Drew's work was still unfinished. Their next chore was breaking up the land that Katie and Adele had just cleared.

"New groun' makes very good corn crops," Alfred told them. "Jes' imagine you're eatin' fresh roas'in' ears an' the work'll seem much easier!"

The boys had difficulty getting much consolation from their father's advice. It was hard to predict which way underground roots were running. Sometimes they could lift the plows to avoid hitting obstacles. Just as often, plowpoints collided with underground roots, forcing plowstocks backwards, or to the left or right, with great force. From collisions affecting various parts of their bodies, Drew and Tom would carry bruise marks and sore muscles for many days.

While their new location proved to be a disappointment, by the year's end more serious world events developed. On December 7, Japan attacked Pearl Harbor, Hawaii. The peacefulness of that bright Sunday morning was dulled by the impact of the surprise bombing by enemy planes.

President Roosevelt declared war the following day. His announcement would dramatically affect many in the days to come, including the Knight family.

Chapter Twenty-Three

Sam made one of his rare visits to see Alfred and Ella one Sunday afternoon. Adele answered the knock on the front door, then stepped back when she opened it to discover her grandfather there. She had expected a girlfriend.

"Where's yer daddy?" Sam asked.

"He's on the back porch with Mother. I'll git him!"

"That's awright. I've got time to talk with you first. We could set over there on the couch."

Unpleasant memories closed in on Adele. "Daddy!" she yelled at the top of her voice.

Alfred hurried to her side, a questioning look on his face. Ella followed close behind. Other children looked around doorways from other rooms in the house.

"What's the matter, Adele?" he asked. "Is sump'n botherin' you?"

Ella gazed perplexedly at her daughter, but said nothing.

It was Sam who spoke next. "Alfred, I need to talk with you privately on the front porch." As father and son left the room, the rest of the family half-heartedly returned to their various activities, straining to hear all they could.

"Things coulda been better 'twixt us. We both know that," Sam began. "I'm sorry for my part'n the matter, an' I'm ready to turn over a new leaf. Viney's goin' to Bosley to live 'an work. She wants to be out on her own. Jake's gittin' married soon. That'll jes leave me an' Mink in my big house, an' I don't b'lieve I can hannel it! If you'll move yer fambly in to hep' me, I'll rentcha the place free."

"Lemme talk it over with Ella, an' I'll letcha know termorrer, Paw."

"Awright, Son," Sam replied, as he arose to leave, and Alfred returned to face his family.

Perhaps the most enticing part of Sam's offer was the rent-free proposition. That appealed to Alfred very much. Katie would appreciate being closer to church again on Sunday mornings. With her brothers and sisters growing up, her greatest responsibility now was watching Will to help him stay balanced, so he wouldn't fall and hurt himself. Walking was a very difficult chore for him. It would be a long time, if ever, before he could handle his own problems.

Ella had reservations about moving in with her husband's father and her disabled brother-in-law. Maybe Sam was repentent at the time, but it might be part of a desperate move to get much-needed aid. She wondered, too, if she would be expected to help bathe and clothe Mink. It could be very embarrassing at times.

Weighing all pros and cons in the matter, the final decision was made to try, at least, to share Sam's house for a year. If it didn't work out, they would move again.

Their decision was hastened by the marriage of Jake to a farm girl, Marlene Seitz, who lived down the road a couple of miles away. A renter house was available for Jake and his new bride to move into. His father gave him the use of much of the furniture and kitchen appliances in his house to assist him and Marlene in getting started. This left space for Alfred and Ella to move their things into Sam's house.

For this transfer, Alfred considered his family now able to handle all problems involved in the resettling. However, he did accept his younger brother's help, since he had been able to assist Jake in moving out following his marriage. He didn't want his brother to feel a long-term obligation to him and insist on repaying him later.

The cows seemed to take the move in stride. They were now older and more gentle, and probably remembered every pothole and turn in the dusty road from the previous resettlings. Even the chickens appeared to struggle less, as though resigned to whatever fate awaited them. The children, of course, had grown older and stronger, and were able to show more patience in dealing with the animals.

Drew, perhaps, was least happy with their latest move. He had made friends in the hollow and would have liked to remain closer to them. They knew all the animal trails through the woods, and shared swimming holes in a nearby creek. In fact, he had often been remiss in doing his share of farm work. It wasn't unusual to find his hoe at the end of a crop row. Sometimes hours passed before he returned to man it again. There was still concern on the part of Drew's parents for his frailty, so he wasn't pressured into working as hard as his brothers and sisters.

Drew's friends came visiting him often at his grandfather's place, and they set out to blaze new trails. The woods behind the church became a favorite hangout. Sometimes they took their rifles and shot at squirrels.

"I hope you won't shoot into their nests!" Ella admonished. "Don't leave the littl'uns orphans!"

To appease his mother, Drew convinced his friends to follow her suggestions. After all, there were other things to shoot at. Some of them had more implications than firing into squirrel nests.

"I bet I can shoot closer to the knob on the back door of the church without hittin' it'n any of you can!" Elmer Small yelled.

"Oh, yeah!" Clarence Gentry replied. "Le's see who's the bes' shot!"

The boys drew straws to see who would fire first, the shortest straw giving the choice spot. The others would take their turns in accordance with the length of their draws.

The game started off well, with plenty of space left between wood and metal. However, as time passed, fear of losing caused a reduction in the margin and resultant damage to the doorknob. The boys retreated to the woods, certain that they had been seen.

They were correct in their fears. A neighbor called the county sheriff in Bosley, who drove out and found them in their hiding place. They were confronted and led to their parents. The promise to replace the knob mechanism, repair other damage, and perform community services saved the boys from spending time in jail. The worst penalty to them was the confiscation of their rifles.

Chapter Twenty-Four

Once routines were established, settling in with Sam and Mink Knight presented no problems, at least at the outset. No change in schools for the children was necessary. Ella's older boys helped their disabled uncle with personal problems if the need arose, and the girls kept their distance from their grandfather. Meals were shared, everyone sitting together at Sam's long dining-room table.

All diners ate less hurriedly so that Will and Mink didn't have to finish alone because of their health-induced slowness. Conversation centered on neighbors, livestock and farm crops. Since Jake had taken the family's animals, Alfred's and Ella's cows and mules were essential to the smooth continued operation of Sam's farm.

Jake, being older and much more experienced with farming, helped Drew and Tom prepare the soil and plant cotton and corn. When Alfred's work day ended at the sawmill, he was able to instruct his sons with the planting items for the family's enjoyment, such as sorghum cane, popcorn, watermelons, and peanuts. The vegetable garden was Ella's and the girls' responsibility after Tom prepared it for planting. Sam Knight tried to keep equipment mended and the weeds cut around the house and barn with his sling blade.

With so much farm work necessitating Tom's and Drew's absence from school, they barely managed to pass their grades. The older girls sometimes missed classes too, to help hoe the fields. Their grades were somewhat higher than their brothers', but they could have been much better under different circumstances.

When the children prayed for rain to keep them out of the fields after school ended and farming became full-time, answered prayers brought little relief. There were usually fencing wire and fence posts to be replaced, and broken terrace rows to be mended following heavy rains. It was also a time for taking mules to the blacksmith to be shod, or corn to the grist mill to be ground into meal.

The more embarrassing task of taking cows to see their male friends when mating time came also had to be dealt with. The boys had to trot to keep the animals from running over them on the trip down the road. It was different on the return tip. The poor cows weren't allowed to visit as long as they would have liked, and had to be practically dragged home. Neighbors along the road snickered when the boys passed by with the beasts.

When school began again, the children attended regularly until cotton bolls opened. Then the back-breaking job of bending to pluck the puffy, white locks from sharp, protective burrs demanded more time away from classes. This, plus sorghum-making and hay-baling, meant considerable schoolwork had to be made up. Later, corn would have to be harvested, bringing on additional homework to catch up in class.

When the Knight kids caught up with their own duties, Alfred offered their services to neighbors at standard rates for jobs done. Sensing an opportunity to earn some money to spend for things they needed, they were very sorely disappointed. Alfred was paid for the work his children did. Instead of passing it on to his sons and daughters, it went into his own pockets. "We'll save this for hard times," he told them. They couldn't picture things being more difficult than they already were.

Katie developed bunions on her toes from wearing shoes too tight for her feet. Adele's shoes were too large, and rubbed blisters on her heels from sliding up and down. When the older boys wore holes in their shoe soles or had rips develop in the seams, they had to keep wearing them. Their clothing was patched so much that it looked like splotched quilts.

When Christmas came, there was only a meager amount of fruit and nuts for presents. Alfred had high hopes of more profitable farming, and his eyes often gazed into the valley below, where more level land would make it easier to use farm machinery. He was saving for that.

That time was hastened when Ella tired of seeing her father-in-law stare at her daughters. She decided to tell Alfred about the earlier incident involving Adele. "Our dog don't even like yer paw. Shag bristles up at him all the time. Don't be rough on him, Alfred. Jes' say we want to move to the valley."

Although it was mid-winter, the decision was made to move right away. It was a good time for the kids to change schools, since it was mid-term break. The tiring job of moving again wasn't anticipated with joy. It meant telling old friends and relatives goodbye, and resettling among strangers.

The single most enjoyable thing about moving was not having to contend with the animals. Since it was too far to walk with cows, mules, and chickens, Alfred made additional trips to transport them in his truck. The family was proud to accomplish their last move without help from Alfred's brothers.

Sam was full of self-pity when they left. "I wish you'd reconsider an' stay!" he pleaded tearfully. "I need y'all!"

Alfred reminded his father that several brothers and sisters were handy to help him, and he thought their being gone would be appreciated later.

Their new valley home was similar to the mountain house in the hollow in some ways. It, too, was on lower terrain. But instead of overlooking a gap in the mountain to the valley below, the land rose abruptly behind the house and continued rising into a mountaintop. From an opening at the base of the rise, a spring of clear, cold water gushed out in bubbly ripples. The front of the house faced land waiting to be plowed and planted. Anticipating huge future profits, Alfred spent his savings for a brand new John Deere tractor. "We'll keep our mules fer plowin' our garden an' soft soil where the tractor might mar down," he said.

The Knight clan had scarcely had time to make new friends at Misty Valley High School before Alfred began keeping Tom and Drew out of school to turn the farmland. Day and night the heavy valley soil was plowed by the two.

The boys took turns at day and night duty, one sleeping while the other worked. When they finished and returned to school, Alfred quit his sawmill job and began breaking land for neighbors. He spent little of his income on his family. His mind was set on acquiring additional farm machinery. "One of these days, I'll have a cornpicker!" he boasted.

"I could fine better things to spen' money on!" Ella thought, as she prepared milk and butter for storing in the cold spring to keep their freshness.

Chapter Twenty-Five

Whether certain preachers recognized a religious tie between the Knights and Alfred's parents and older sister, or saw an opportunity to add a sizeable family to their membership rolls, their frequent visits promised much.

"We're like one big, happy family!" Church of Christ pastor, Ervin Thorpe, told them. "Everyone pitches in when someone has problems!"

When Alfred began looking forward to visits from the minister, Ella was elated. Although she had grown up as a Southern Baptist, she appreciated any decision on her husband's part that would make him a better person. None of the family had attended church in the two months they had lived in the valley. When Alfred agreed to begin going to church, Ella hoped activities there would completely take his mind off other women. She would soon know.

Katie welcomed her parents starting to attend church with her. It was a restless time for them the first Sunday. They had to consider those around them and quell certain mannerisms common to them at home. "I hope Daddy don't belch out loud!" Adele whispered to Tom.

Katie felt that certain chains were released when Will and Minnie Vee took their seats between their parents. She had trouble adjusting to her lack of responsibility for her younger brother and sister.

At the end of the church service, everyone came around to greet the family. Alfred and Ella beamed from the attention they received.

The preacher convinced Alfred that his church was set apart in the Bible as a choice institution. His reference to all the times "Church of Christ" was mentioned in holy scripture made Ella wonder if the good man might not be interpreting the words wrong, but she needed to feel it was true for Alfred's sake.

"Why didn't they play the piano when we sung?" Norma asked after they returned home. "Aunt Minnie always played fer singin' in the other church!"

"Maw tole me once that we're s'posed to make a joyful noise in our heart." Alfred replied.

"The only noise my heart makes is 'dee-dump, dee-dump, dee-dump'!" Nathan exclaimed.

"But don'tcha feel like it might be singin' a silent song sometimes, Nathan?" his mother asked.

"Jes' when a purty girl smiles at me!"

"Didjer heart sing a happy song today when the purty little girl across the aisle kep' smilin' at you, Katie?" Norma asked.

Katie was somewhat embarrassed. "It didn't affect me that way, but I think me 'an her'll be frien's. I'd already met her in school. Her name's Nellie Plummer."

"I'm purty sure she's gonna be my sweetheart!" Drew declared.

"When didja decide that, son?" Alfred asked.

"I guess I musta felt that silent singin' inside me the firs' time I saw her on the school bus!"

"That's sure fas' action!" Tom added.

To show her appreciation of Katie, Nellie became a frequent visitor in the Knight household. Their talk centered on teachers and fellow students at Misty Valley High School. When they began talking about cute boys, Nellie didn't have much to say about anyone except Drew.

When Katie asked permission to visit Nellie, her parents consented for her to go only if Drew accompanied her. This greatly pleased and delighted him. Normally he didn't appreciate going with his sisters anywhere. This occasion was a different matter. All qualities Nellie had appeared to blend with his. Their attraction for each other seemed to have been predestined.

Nellie didn't have a brother to get Katie's attention. This fact was quite prominent in Katie's parents' decision to let her visit. There was only one sister, two years older than Nellie.

The affection Lyle Plummer showed his daughters was impressive to Katie. She realized how much happier her childhood might have been if her own father had shown a genuine caring attitude toward her.

Before the visit ended, Katie's friend had deserted her for Drew. It was no big concern to Katie, because she had taken such a liking to Nellie's parents. Lillian Plummer was just as friendly as her husband was. Although Lola was somewhat retarded, she was nice in a childish way.

Nellie's future Sunday afternoon visits to see Katie usually began with her asking about Drew. Unless he was wandering around with neighborhood boys, he usually managed to take Nellie aside for some private conversation and "castle building" with her.

Ella didn't let them out of her sight for long at a time. Everyone talked about the young girl on the mountain who had a baby out of wedlock. She didn't want her son to be responsible for a similar problem.

"Whether clean or tarnished, it looks like Drew's gonna be the firs' to leave our nes'," Ella confided to her husband.

Chapter Twenty-Six

When school began at Misty Valley in September, Ella was apprehensive about enrolling Will. His steps were erratic and unsteady, his speech distorted, and his movements jerky. She wondered how the other students would react to him. Would he be accepted, or scorned and ridiculed?

She walked with him and his siblings to meet the school bus. "Katie, I want you to go to Will's class with him an' he'p him git to know his teacher an' git usta his surroundin's!"

"Yes, ma'm." Katie replied dutifully.

When they arrived at school, Katie's brothers and sisters went their separate ways, while she escorted Will to his classroom. Students they met in the hallway stared at Will curiously, but few made any unkind remarks. There were some low-voiced comments. "What's the matter with him?" "Why does he ack lak he does?"

Katie ignored unfavorable remarks as much as possible. Looking straight ahead, she led Will to the end of the hallway where the first grade classroom was located.

She introduced Will to his teacher, Miss Stroud, and explained his problems to her as best she could.

"I think we'll get along just fine!" Miss Stroud replied, stroking Will's blond, curly hair.

"You dah haffa peh me!" Will protested. "Ah nah ah daw!" He backed quickly away from his teacher.

"Sorry! I didn't mean to mess up your hair!" Miss Stroud apologized, choosing to ignore Will's remarks, or not understand him.

Then she turned to Katie. "Why don't you run along to your own classes, honey? We'll take good care of your brother!"

Although Katie did as the teacher suggested, and didn't see Will until school dismissed, her mind was on him throughout the day.

That evening, Will had much to talk about. Miss Stroud, it seemed, had centered her attentions on him throughout the day, and had made certain the other students fully understood his problems.

"She seh Ah huh Leh Gree Gah!" Will boasted. Ella wondered why Miss Stroud had chosen to put her handicapped child on a pedestal.

Perhaps Alfred's father had mellowed with age. At least, that's what Ella hoped when they accepted an invitation from him to return to his place for a Sunday family dinner.

"Everybody's bringing a pot of food," Sam's postcard had read. "Come on up after church and enjoy visiting with yer brothers and sisters."

Moving off the mountain into the valley had isolated them from kinfolks. Everyone looked forward to the reunion.

What Alfred hadn't anticipated was that some of his nephews would bring their male friends along. Otherwise, he might have elected to keep his family home.

Since there was more parking space available in Sam's front yard than his, Jake parked the school bus he drove on his father's property.

As the afternoon wore on, the natural attraction between male and female teenagers made itself known. They sought separation from their elders in the school bus, shielded from the sun by a large sycamore tree.

When Alfred realized his older daughters were out of sight, he left the house to look around. It didn't take long for him to spot them sitting in the back of the school bus with their cousins and their friends. He wasted no time in approaching Katie and Adele.

"You gals had better git offa this bus!" Alfred announced, as he jerked the door open. "I'm not runnin' a whorehouse!"

As the teenagers scattered, Katie's and Adele's eyes were filled with tears. They felt embarrassed and belittled by their father's harsh and unjustified remarks. They spent the remainder of their visit in company with their female cousins.

As her family prepared to return home to the valley, Ella suggested they drive to the other side of the mountain to see her mother for a few minutes.

Nelda and Otha were sitting silently on their front porch when they drove up. Ella's sister was looking through a Sears and Roebuck catalog, and her mother was staring into space, motionless.

After bringing Ella up-to-date regarding her other children and their families, Nelda inquired about the welfare of Alfred's and Ella's kids.

"They're awright an' in school," Ella answered. "We jes hafta be extry careful about the boys our girls choose to mix with."

"If they was mine," Nelda quickly responded, "I'd put a chas'ty belt on 'em!"

If Ella had hoped for a less critical attitude on her mother's part, she was grossly disappointed. She was ready to go home!

"Can you b'lieve Maw's ole timey notions?" Ella asked Alfred, as they were returning home with their children riding to the back of the truck.

"Yeah, I sure can!" Alfred replied, unflinchingly.

Chapter Twenty-Seven

Misty Valley High School brought in students from a wide area. An advantage of teaching the same youths for all grades was the ability to follow their progress from first grade to high school graduation. Any problems could be discussed easily with a future teacher.

Katie wondered if her father would ever allow her to have a boyfriend. She hid any thoughts she had for boys in her shy behavior, and turned to sports as an outlet for her pent-up feelings. She became a team leader in softball and basketball.

The only way Alfred permitted her to play games away from school at times other than day schedules was to accompany her. Her brothers and sisters, with the exception of Will and Minnie Vee, joined her father in cheering her on. She played much harder to please them and receive their applause. She dared not do otherwise.

"If I play bad," she guessed, "Daddy'll put me down in fronta ever'body!"

Softball games were all played while school was in session. Katie was quite relaxed batting or holding down her first base position. "What if I make a mistake or two?" she consoled herself. "Daddy's not aroun' to embarrass me!"

Perhaps she practiced too hard when preparing for basketball games. One day while dribbling the ball as she rushed toward the goal, her feet slipped on the polished floor of the gym, and she fell and hit her head on the hard surface.

As she lay dazed on the floor, her coach and fellow players gathered around her, fanning her with hats and caps, trying to get her back on her feet.

"How many fingers do you see in front of you?" the coach asked, holding up his right hand with all fingers extended.

"Four," Katie replied.

"Are you sure?"

"Yes."

"Look again!"

"I still see four fingers!"

"Are you counting this one?" he asked, wiggling his thumb.

"That's not a finger!" Katie replied. "That's a thumb!"

Realizing his own specific mistake, the flushed coach continued. "You seem to be okay, Katie, but I think I oughta drive you home!"

"I'll be okay." Katie tried to assure him. "I can manage til school's out."

Coach Draper was young and handsome. His blue eyes and blond, wavy hair got the attention of all the teenaged girls. If Katie permitted him to take her home, her father would probably stop her from playing in any more basketball games. Besides, her fellow students would kid her for special considerations he showed her.

As she walked unsteadily down the hallway and to the day's remaining class, Katie was glad to have Nellie by her side to keep her from wobbling too much.

When Katie bumped hard into the door-facing as they entered English class, Nellie chastised her for not letting Coach Draper take her home. "You sure missed out by not lettin' that han'some hunk take you home. What a lotta us girls would've give to have had that opportunity. He tickles all of our fancies, you know!"

"How could you say that, Nellie? Coach Draper's a nice man! Besides, you ought'nt to think pas' my brother; that is, if you plan to marry him like you tole me the other day!"

"Drew ain't give me no ring, yet. So I don't consider myself totally his! I'm glad to have the freedom to still look aroun', jes' in case our plans don't work out. An' Coach Draper's sure good fer my eyes!"

Although Katie found some of Nellie's talk shocking, she envied her ability to act on her own. She often wished she could make more of her own decisions. Her parents might want her to be an old maid schoolteacher, but she wasn't sure she wanted that!

"I would never have anybody to call me Mother!" she speculated. "Nobody would be near to snuggle up to when nights was cold, or to wade in the cool waters of a creek with me on hot summer days!" She wondered what would happen to her if her parents died and left her alone in the house.

She didn't realize how deep in thoughts she had become submerged until she felt Nellie's elbow in her side. Then she became aware that her teacher was asking her a question.

"Wouldja repeat the question, Miz Cates?" she asked, startled.

"I've already asked you twice! What's a good affirmative reply to a truth-seeking question?"

"Yes," Katie replied, haphazardly.

"Very nice!" Mrs. Cate's comments stunned her.

"You can be very smart if you put forth the effort, Katie." Mrs. Cates continued. "You just need to be aware of what's going on around you!"

"I've been doin' that alla my life!" Katie whispered to Nellie.

Chapter Twenty-Eight

Alfred's imagination carried him well past the bounds of reality. He envisioned Katie and Adele becoming boy-crazy to the point that they would be aggressive, throwing themselves at young men. His own experiences had proved to him that such young women aren't respected. He certainly didn't want any illegitimate grandchildren running around in his house.

He took the matter up with his preacher. "Brother Thorpe, what does the Bible say about women who're too familiar with men?"

"Well, the penalty is pretty severe. Stoning was commonly used."

"Does that mean, if it gits necessary, I oughta take my girls out in the fiel' an' throw rocks at 'em?"

"Why are you so concerned, Alfred? Your daughters seem real nice to me!"

"Oh, they ain't done nothin' bad yet. They've jes' started leanin' in that d'rection. I wanna take the right steps when it happ'ns!"

"Maybe it won't ever happen."

"I've got a feeln' it might some day, irregardless of what I do to try to stop it!"

"What makes you think that?"

"Las' Sunday, while our fambly was visitin' Paw, I missed Katie an' Adele. The older kids had got real quiet, so I figgered sump'n was up. Sure enough, I foun' 'em settin' on a school bus with some boys they'd never met before. I thought it was real brazen!"

"We should certainly be aware at all times where our young folks are and what they're doing. Were they hugging and kissing, holding hands, or just sitting and talking?

"They was jes' settin' an' talkin' when I got close to the bus. I donno what mighta happ'ned earlier!"

"It probably won't ever happen, but if your girls ever get into trouble, we'll have them confess at church in front of the whole congregation. Usually that sets their thinking straight, and no other action is necessary."

"Thanks fer the advice, Bro. Thorpe. I'll talk this matter over with my girls."

When Alfred took Katie and Adele aside after supper that evening to explain his conversation with the preacher, they couldn't understand why their father felt it necessary to say what he did.

"I wantcha both to know aheada time what to expeck if you ever let things get outta han' between you and yer boyfriends!" he concluded.

While Katie and Adele washed dishes, they talked in low voices about their father's suspicious mind.

"He must've seen lotsa women like Carol Biddy in his wile days. Now that he's slowed down, he prob'bly wonders what caused 'em to be that way!" Adele surmised.

"Yeah, and he imagines our wile streaks've started to show." Katie added.

"Maybe I oughta change my name to Mimi the Man Trap," Adele said, "an' you could be Francine the Fox!"

Although the whole matter concerned them greatly, the two girls began to giggle while thinking of the vast difference between them and the characters they imagined.

Katie hadn't completely regained her composure when she approached the metal cabinet with a final armload of dishes she had just rinsed. She set them on a shelf and was turning away, when the cabinet came crashing down behind her. She obviously hadn't secured them adequately. Everything in the storage shelves was broken.

The whole family rushed into the kitchen to see what had happened. "Are y'all awright?" Tom asked, very much concerned.

"Yes," his sisters answered, huddled in a corner, frightened by the noise as well as the prospects of an impending scolding.

"Y'all know we don't have the money fer more dishes!" Ella shouted. "I donno what we'll eat out of!"

"If you'd been payin' more attention to yer work, this wouldn't've happn'd!" Alfred chastised them.

"If we end up eatin' outta the trough with the hogs, don't complain!"

Ella was enraged. "Clean up yer mess an' dump it outside in the weeds!"

As they took the broken dishes outside as directed, Adele whispered to Katie: "D'you think she'll really march us all off to the pig pen an' serve our meals in the trough?"

"Nothin' would surprise me anymore." Katie replied softly.

While the kids were in school the next day, Ella visited the hall pantry to see if she could find any spare dishes there. The search was futile. However, an idea came to her. "Why cain't we use pint fruit jars fer drinkin' glasses an' syrup bucket lids fer plates?" She found a considerable number of those items. "Our fambly could stan' more humblin' anyhow!"

Late that afternoon, the children having prepared their lessons for the next day, and the evening meal cooking on the stove, Alfred marched in to say the preacher was going to join the family for supper.

"Why didn't you lemme know sooner, Alfred, so I could've fixed sump'n special?" Ella asked.

"I didn't know about it aheada time, myself. I met the preacher on my way home and he sorta invited hisself."

"Well, we'll make out. We'll jes hafta spread the food out thinner!"

Katie and Adele were quite shaken with the announcement. "I hate to face that man after what Daddy tole him!" Katie admitted.

"I feel the same," Adele agreed. "We'll jes' hafta hol' our heads up high."

"An' git ridyculed fer that?"

"Well, le's jes' try to ack like we're calm an' cool."

"I'll try!" Katie agreed.

After the preacher entered and greeted the family, he approached Katie and Adele. "How're you girls doing?" His piercing eyes made them feel uncomfortable.

"Awright," they replied shyly.

At this point, Ella brought out her pint fruit jars and syrup bucket lids. "Katie an' Adele broke all our dishes, an' this is all we've got to eat outta!"

Katie's and Adele's embarrassment was now impossible to hide. They ran from the room, crying.

Chapter Twenty-Nine

The preacher obviously spread word around about the Knight family's shortage of dishes. Soon after his impromptu visit, members of his congregation began dropping by from time to time with glasses of jelly, plates of melon, and bowls of pie or other treats. They each made it known that they didn't want their dishes returned. Katie and Adele began feeling more kindly toward those around them. It was great to have good friends!

Alfred bought a sorghum mill and began encouraging his acquaintances to include sorghum cane among their crops, so he could process it for them. The future looked very promising for his business.

Late spring and summer were busy times. Alfred felt he must practice what he preached, so his crops included a patch of sorghum cane, too. With cotton as the main money crop, he could foresee a profitable future. He had his sons set aside forty acres for the fiber-yielding plants. All the children old enough to drive the tractor, or strong enough to handle a hoe, were busy in the fields.

Katie and Adele were given sole responsibility for keeping grass and weeds out of the cotton fields. With blisters on their hands, and sweating from their labors, they trudged home at sunset each day to additional cleaning duties in the kitchen.

The loneliness of the fields was made more tolerable by the companionship of their faithful collie. Shag acted as their protector, chasing away any creature that showed up in their patch.

One day the girls took a brief rest in the shade of trees bordering the field. Shag busied himself in the nearby woods, running in and out of bushes in search of rabbits. When he suddenly backed away, barking excitedly, Adele went to investigate. She ran back to Katie with a terrified look on her face.

"Let's get outta here, Katie. Shag's foun' the bigges' rattler I ever saw!"

"Cain't we kill it with our hoes?"

"No, it's too big, Katie. We might miss, an' it'd bite us fer sure!"

"Le's call for he'p! Maybe Tom or Drew'll hear us an come to see what's wrong!"

They ran into the field for a few paces and began yelling as loud as they could, "He'p! He'p! Shag's foun' a rattlesnake!"

When they received no indication their shouts had been heard, Katie and Adele ran toward the distant cornfield where their brothers and sisters were working. Their siblings stared at them as they kicked up dust in their hasty approach.

"What in the worl's the matter!" Tom asked, as he turned off the tractor's engine.

"Shag's bayed a whopper of a rattler, an' it's too big fer us to mess with!" Adele shouted, breathlessly.

"Was the snake mad? Was it singin'?" Tom asked.

"It looked mad, but it wasn't singin'. It couldn't, 'cause it had a frog in its mouth!" Adele replied.

Tom's laughter annoyed the frightened sisters. How could he be jovial at a time like this? "Was it singin' with its rattlers?"

"I donno. Shag was makin' so much noise with his barkin'!"

Their siblings followed close behind, as Katie and Adele ran back across the field to the woods where Shag was still barking furiously.

The rattler had managed to swallow the frog and was now striking viciously at Shag, as he circled the serpent in search of a vulnerable area of its body to attack.

"Good boy, Shag!" Tom called the dog away so he could deal a mortal blow to the snake. After killing the rattlesnake, he gave its rattles to Adele to keep for a souvenir of "the snake that couldn't sing."

Adele placed the rattles on a small log to dry, and everyone returned to work. "I hope that rascal's mate's not lurkin' close by!" she remarked.

Once the cultivation season was over, sorghum cane matured and was brought by customers and deposited near Alfred's sorghum mill, rising in high stacks.

Manning the various sections of the mill required the help of many family members. Tom and Drew hitched one of their father's mules to the pole attached to the mill wheels that crushed the stalks of cane as the wheels turned.

The speed of the crushing wheels depended on the gait of the mule pulling the pole in a wide circle. While the animal wasn't kept in a gallop, he was constantly urged on to speed up the work. Drew handed a dozen or so stalks at a time to Tom, who fed them into the wheels, then threw the refuse aside. His younger brothers and sisters piled the spent stalks into a growing heap.

Greenish-yellow juice ran from the mill wheels into a trough that carried the savory liquid to cooking pans. There Alfred channeled the juice from one section of the pans into another, until it thickened into the required consistency. Nathan kept the logs piled on the fire that cooked the juice into syrup.

Finally, Ella put lids on filled buckets and stacked them up, keeping one of very four as payment for the syrup-making service.

Profit from the procedure was considerable, but when young men began eyeing his daughters, Alfred decided he wouldn't pursue sorghum-making another year.

Chapter Thirty

Alfred used a portion of his profits from sorghum-making to buy a Philco radio. He was among the first in his community to have one. At first, the radio was a pleasurable device for the family, providing news service, hillbilly and gospel music, and soap operas, so named for their advertisers, but providing story material in prose rather than music.

As the children told their friends about Saturday night music presentations, and their friends told others, soon the Knight home was overflowing with self-invited Saturday evening guests seeking free entertainment. This continued until Ella conveniently dropped the radio and broke it.

Katie and Adele remembered the words and music to many tunes, both hillbilly and gospel, they had heard while still having their radio to enjoy. They harmonized songs as they washed and dried dishes. The cotton fields echoed with their renditions, as they finished picking the harvest from their forty acres. Despite the hard work, these songs lifted their spirits above the monotony and tiresomeness of their daily labors.

Accounts told by fellow students of excursions to an overhanging bluff on the mountainside caused the Knight youngsters to want to investigate. Fort Dare, so they were told, got its name from a young Indian couple who had some disagreements. When the pretty princess threatened to jump off the cliff, the prince dared her to do so, thinking she wouldn't go through with it. When she leaped, it settled the argument, severing their relationship and ending her life.

As Katie and her brothers and sisters visited the overlook, they could imagine how peaceful it would be to float over the beautiful valley below. Norma wondered if the princess might have launched her flight unmindful of the wrenching jolt that would end it. "Now that you've visited the place, don't plan to go back fer a while," Alfred told his children. "Bad things go on up there, an' it's bes' you stay away!"

Darlene Proctor lived in the valley directly below Fort Dare. She received a high-powered telescope for Christmas, and had much to tell her friends and classmates about things she had observed through its lenses. "I couldn't b'lieve the drinkin' an' carryin' on I saw takin' place up there!"

"Didja see anybody you knowed?" Katie asked.

"I sure did, an' it surprised me. I learnt some people ain't near as nice as they preten' to be!"

"Have you seen anybody we know?" Adele joined the questioners.

"Well, you ain't lived in the valley long enough to know a lotta the people aroun' here. But somma the fo'ks here know some on the mountain. Maybe because they git aroun' so much. I saw Carol Biddy up there late one afternoon."

"Who was she with?" Adele asked.

"I can't say fer sure, but he looked a lot like yer daddy!"

Katie and Adele made excuses and left the small gathering immediately. They had hoped their father had quit seeing his old flame and had forgotten his past with her. Darlene's conversation cast more shadows on his character.

"She didn't say how long ago this happ'ned. Maybe it was before he started goin' to church!" Katie said.

"We hope so!" Adele replied.

Things had been more peaceful at home, although everyone continued to be overworked, with no apparent compensation other than the food and clothing they received as part of the family. Katie and Adele vowed never to tell their mother what Darlene had told them.

Alfred saw a dream of his own come true when he accumulated enough money to buy a corn picker. Such equipment would have been unfeasible had they continued to live on the mountain, where the land was too rolling for heavy machinery.

While his offspring worked in the fields picking cotton and gathering corn, Alfred was busy away from home harvesting corn for neighbors with his tall machine. His billfold bulged with cash he was reluctant to share with his family.

Ella suspected Alfred gambled with his money when the opportunity arose. Perhaps, too, he insisted on buying refreshments when he conversed with neighbors at the nearby country store. She wished he had a shed for his tractor and corn picker. She hated to see them rust away from setting outside in the many pouring rains that drenched the valley.

True to his word, Alfred sold his sorghum mill. It became another segment of the passing scenes in family history. With the burning of the pile of spent cane stalks, only memories remained of pleasant associations around the old mill. That remembrance was renewed each time the delicious syrup it produced remained an important part of the breakfast meal.

Alfred began looking for another place to rent. It was as through he felt that changing houses would interfere with the schemes of young men to establish relationships with his attractive girls.

Katie liked where they lived. She would miss the upstairs retreat, where rare moments alone had given her the opportunity to survey the surrounding countryside from its protruding windows. She wondered what might happen to family members with the passage of time. Would there ever be stability for any of them?

Wherever they moved, several months remained for them in their present home. There were still fields of cotton to be picked and acres of corn to be brought in before late fall rains set in. Also, once colder weather arrived, their hogs would be butchered, lard rendered from the fatty portions, and the lean cuts salted and stored away.

With so many days missed from school to help with farm work, the children struggled to make passing grades. It was their most difficult school year. "When will we ever stop workin' so hard so Daddy can have rusty machinery?" Tom asked his mother one day.

Ella's reply was blunt and definite. "Don't ever question yer daddy's judgment!"

Norma had a flair for decorating. As Christmas neared, she thought it would be a delight to spruce the place up as a going-away present. Parts of her plan were easy to comply with. Holly was plentiful on the banks of nearby creeks and mistletoe thrived on numerous old trees.

The boys enjoyed excursions to bring in red-berried sprigs, and using their rifles to bring down mistletoe clusters was fun.

Since money wasn't available to buy tree ornaments, popcorn was strung on branches of a well-proportioned cedar. Cutouts from the Sears and Roebuck catalog provided other tree ornaments. Pieces of colorful cloth discards provided room stringers. The old house had probably never experienced such sprucing up. Norma was justifiably proud of her handiwork.

Chapter Thirty-One

Alfred gathered his family around him to tell them about his future plans. "Spud Willmer has offered to rent us his stone house nex' year. It'll be jes' about the bes' place to live we've ever had. The lan' is on a rise an' drains good. Even though our country's at war, we oughta be able to whip the Japs an' the Germans soon an' not hafta put up with rationin' much more."

He went on to say that some of their new neighbors-to-be could use extra help in the fields. "Drew an' Tom, you can bring in extry money by hirin' out durin' the plantin' an' harvestin' seasons. The resta the fambly can keep our own work up. Later on, maybe we can sen' Katie to Drummond College so she can study to be a school teacher. Adele can fine a job in Bosley while Katie's away an' bring her money home. You younger kids'll hafta put out more in the fiel's to he'p the older ones git away from home later."

Ella was defensive of Will. He had become stronger as he matured, but he would never overcome his birth injuries. He continued to walk with a shuffle. When he reached for something, his hands jerked back, and his speech was slurred. "D'you think you can hannel a man's share of the farm work?" she asked him.

"Shooh," he replied, flexing his arm muscles, "Ah stroh nuff do mah woh!"

Ella shook her head, but made no further comments. She knew Will couldn't be pushed. If he were rushed, he would become even more nervous and unsteady.

"Can I keep the money I make workin' fer other people?" Tom asked.

"I donno why not." his father replied.

Drew was less enthusiastic. He had never cared for hard work. While he enjoyed tinkering with motors to keep them running, he had trouble motivating himself otherwise. "If Uncle Sam'll leave me alone, I'll be a married man soon!" he declared.

"I guess we'll hafta plan without you, Drew," Alfred resumed. "If Uncle Sam don't gitcha, Nellie prob'bly will!"

The younger children asked if they would also be able to work away from home to make money after they moved.

"I don't think so," Alfred answered. "You'll hafta fill the gaps lef' by the others!"

Now seventeen, Katie could foresee another hard year ahead of her before any prospects of change. She couldn't imagine her father paying for her to attend college. If he had the money, he would be reluctant to spend it that way.

Tom had never earned his own money. He had always worked for the family, never having cash to spend as he saw fit. The thought of having his own spending money was overwhelming.

Adele couldn't picture Alfred letting her go to Bosley and work. There was the possibility of her meeting a nice young man who would sweep her off her feet. And her father wouldn't be around to keep it from happening!

Nathan and Norma saw no excuse for any celebrating. All they saw ahead were sweat, blisters, and tired legs and backs.

As the youngest in the family, Minnie Vee felt she would be looked after, regardless of what happened to the others. If she just whimpered, everyone came running to see what was wrong with her. When she blamed someone else for bothering her, that person had better have a good answer. Her parents seemed to think she never did anything wrong.

There were times, though, when she preferred to make her own decisions. Her older brothers and sisters knew their parents well enough to know that the day would come when their little sister could well be a prisoner in her own home. Alfred and Ella might well become so protective of her that the time they allowed her to spend away from them might be almost nonexistent.

Her mother assumed the principal responsibility for her. When Minnie Vee was younger, she often took naps with her father. One day she questioned Ella as to why Alfred's body was different from hers.

Although Ella explained that God made men and women that way so they could wear the clothes they wore, she stopped Minnie Vee from sleeping with Alfred to avoid future questions.

Chapter Thirty-Two

Moving day, which had become routine, went smoothly. Within a few hours, everything was again in place in the new location. Although the rooms in the house were small, there was plenty of sleeping space for four kids to a bedroom. The sturdy concrete floor was easy to keep clean.

Once everyone was settled in, the task of turning the soil and readying it for planting began. A raw, east wind rumpled Tom's shirt night after night, and a threatening March sky urged him on before spring storms arrived with their heavy rains to make the ground too wet to plow or too soft to support the weight of the heavy tractor.

Nathan was now old enough to help with the work. An extra person in the fields allowed more time in the classrooms for Drew and Tom. It was Nathan who had to adjust to making up schoolwork.

When their own plowing was finished for the present time, Alfred approached Tom about helping a neighbor catch up. "Ole man Jenks has been sick an' has lotsa lan' still to break. He says he'll pay three dollars a day fer he'p. I tole him you might do it."

"I guess I can stan' to lose a little more time from school," Tom replied. "That's purty good money!"

While the other boys returned to school, Tom followed a mule all day behind a turning plow. Alfred was using his tractor to help another neighbor. When the job was done and Tom received no compensation, he questioned his father about the pay.

"Mr. Jenks asked if he could settle in the fall when he sells his cotton. I tole him we could wait."

Disappointed, Tom returned to school and the difficult task of making up lost time.

Drew faced another problem. It had been several months since he had registered for the draft upon turning eighteen. When the postman delivered a letter from the draft board requesting him to report for a physical examination, he had mixed feelings. If he were inducted, the opportunity to see different parts of the world was exciting.

When Nellie heard about the letter, she wailed so loudly that it disturbed her neighbors a half a mile away. They came to investigate and found Nellie's parents trying to console her. She wasn't convinced it would be a short war and Drew would soon return.

"What if he's killed?!" she screamed.

"You're cryin' too early, honey." Her mother tried to reason with her. "He may not pass his physical!"

"He's as good as in!" Nellie continued sobbing. "He's about as healthy as a horse!"

Perhaps the frustration of the whole matter got to Drew. At any rate, he often slipped away from his field work and was gone for several hours at a time before returning.

On one occasion, Katie had worked hard all day hoeing cotton. When she came in from the fields, her mother was trying to finish patching some overalls for the boys. She asked Katie to cook supper.

Before the food finished cooking, Drew returned home hungry. He complained about supper not being ready.

Katie, resenting his slothfulness in the field and already exhausted before beginning to prepare the meal, lashed out with a verbal outburst. "I'll be glad when the Army gits you!"

Katie's words stung Drew. Striking back, he landed a blow with his fist on the side of her head. Stunned and injured, she fell to the floor.

Dazed, she struggled to her feet and tried to regain her balance. Ella left her sewing to investigate the commotion.

"Drew jes' about knocked me out with his fis'!" Katie sobbed.

"She said she'd be glad when I went to the Army! She hadn't oughta said that!"

"No, she oughtn't!" Ella agreed.

Getting a limb from a willow in the backyard, Ella gave Katie a few hefty licks with it.

Before long, Drew passed his physical and was inducted into the Army. Katie's vision was still blurred from the blow he gave her as she watched him wave to the family before he climbed aboard the bus bound for camp.

Chapter Thirty-Three

Although it was evident something was wrong with Katie, no effort was made to seek medical attention. She had difficulty walking a straight line, and her headaches were persistent.

Alfred felt that she had become allergic to sunlight, so he excused her from morning work in the fields. Instead, he told her to help Ella with housework.

The headaches continued, but they were more bearable inside the house. However, Katie found the work just as tiring. Afternoons in the fields were less of an ordeal only because of the morning reprieve.

Tom had the opportunity to help Mr. Jenks again in the fall with gathering in his corn crop. When the work was finished, Tom was told that Alfred would get the money to pass on to him.

Christmas neared, and Tom kept waiting for his father to hand over the cash for his spring and fall labors. There were some cowboy boots in a Bosley store he had anticipated buying for months.

Finally, Tom could stand being put off no more. "Daddy," he asked, "did Mr. Jenks ever han' you money to give me fer the work I done fer him?"

Clearing his throat, Alfred replied. "I meant to tell you, Son. Guess I jes' plain forgot. My cornpicker needed fixin', so I used the money. You'll git it later!"

Tom couldn't guess how much longer he would have to wait, but he hoped not for long.

Nellie came over for a visit, elated. Drew had been shipped to England and mailed her an engagement ring as soon as he had saved enough from his paychecks to buy it. It was a half-carat diamond in sterling silver. Ella imagined her son spent all the money he had on it.

Katie often went outside the house, away from the others, when she could. With everyone seeming to talk at the same time, the sounds echoed in her head. Wearing a broad-brimmed straw hat for protection from the sun, she enjoyed sitting under two willows in the back yard.

Sometimes the trees appeared to appreciate her presence, reaching out with their trailing branches and tenderly wrapping them around her. She wanted to repay them, but didn't know how to do so.

The limb from which Ella had broken the switch to punish Katie following her disagreement with Drew had scaled over, like a scab that forms on a sore trying to heal. During her visit, Katie kissed it instinctively, feeling pity for its struggle.

As she was returning to the house, a sudden breeze bent the tree toward her, making it appear that she was being thanked for her concern.

During future visits to the willows, they often dragged their slender leaves across her shoulders, as though caressing them. "Bless you!" Katie whispered, imagining they had ears to hear.

When Tom told his mother he would be glad when he was old enough to join the Navy, she was startled. "I thought you'd be satisfied to wait fer the draft, since you're gittin' to work out on yer own."

"It's not what I expected," Tom confessed. "I thought I'd git paid fer my work!"

"Didn't you?"

"I ain't seen a cent of it yet!"

"D'you know why?"

"Daddy tole me he needed it fer cornpicker repairs."

"Well, you'll git repaid sooner or later. Yer daddy has lotsa upkeep problems!"

"I'm havin' problems feelin' appreciated." Tom confessed. "I guess you could say it's gittin' to be a question of 'keep' instead of 'upkeep' with me!"

Chapter Thirty-Four

"Maybe I'll git all the money at Christmas that Mr. Jenks paid Daddy fer my work," Tom hoped. "It'd be a nice bunnel of cash to git at one time!"

When Christmas came, his father made no mention of the back wages. Tears welled up in Tom's eyes. He was too manly to cry openly, although he felt like doing so. He couldn't understand how his father could be so heartless about the matter. His birthday was two months away, and his mind was made up in regard to the troubling situation.

On a trip into Bosley, Tom visited the Navy Recruiting Office and picked up some literature. In his spare moments, he read about all the exotic places many ships visit. He was impressed by the pictures of beautiful girls of different nationalities. The many opportunities to establish lasting friendships with other men were also enticing. He would be seventeen soon, and he anticipated the magic date!

February arrived, and so did Tom's birthday. As usual, there was no cake or gifts. Instead, Tom had a going-away surprise for his family.

He had been secretly packing a canvas bag with personal items Navy recruits are asked to bring with them when they report for duty. He had even arranged for a ride into Bosley with a friend, so he wouldn't be dependent upon his family for anything.

The Monday for his planned departure came. Unaware of Tom's plans, Alfred was readying the tractor for him to use for the usual spring land turning.

Tom joined him in the back yard. "Don't count on my he'p this year, Daddy. I've joined the Navy an' am leavin' today!"

"Wait a minute, Son! Don't be hasty. Le's talk this matter over. I've been countin' on you fer lotsa he'p in the fiel' agin this year!"

"You'll jes' hafta depen' on somebody else. My paperwork's all done, an' I'm ready to go!"

Ella overheard portions of the conversation through the open kitchen window. She came outside to join her husband and son. "Tom, think about what you're doin'! The war's windin' down. Chances are you'll never git drafted. I've already got one son in service. That's enough!"

The sound of a car horn on the road in front of the house was Tom's signal to leave. His friend was waiting for him. Picking up the canvas bag, Tom started walking toward the road. Alfred and Ella followed close behind.

As the car sped away, Tom waved briefly to his parents and his brothers and sisters, who had lined up on the front porch to see him leave. In their agony, Alfred and Ella ran down the road behind the car, yelling "Come back, Son! Come back, Son!" But Tom kept going!

With a shortage of male help, the girls were called on to assist with planting the crops. Responsibilities of Nathan as the oldest male child around increased considerably.

School ended, and Katie and Nellie were part of the graduating class of seniors. They each received letters from Drummond College inviting them to enter school there, outlining work opportunities available to pay for tuition and housing.

Both girls wanted to attend. Their parents agreed to let them go, since they would be there together.

Katie was elated, but apprehensive. She had never been away from her parents' watchful eyes. Adjustment would not be easy!

She went outside to sit under the willow trees and meditate. Inside the house, her mother was crying and her father was pacing the floor. A rooster crowed nearby and the cows mooed. Katie wondered if they were celebrating or sorrowing.

Then she felt drops of water on her bare arms, although the sky was completely clear. The willows were weeping! She wondered if they were tears of joy or sorrow. She imagined they were happy for her.

When a strong gust of wind lifted their graceful branches upwards, and the mists increased, she was sure the willows were rejoicing over her planned escape from the chains of farm slavery she had worn so long. Her spontaneous tears mingled with theirs!

About the Author

Dalton Stephenson grew up in the foothills of Northeast Alabama following the years of the Great Depression. The youngest in a farm family of nine children, he attended Whiton Junior High, and Geraldine and Albertville High Schools.

His career began as a teacher with the DeKalb County school system, which he entered immediately after his graduation from Athens College, where he received a B.S. Degree in Commerce. After four years, he began working with the United States Steel Corporation, where he remained until retirement.

His family consists of three married daughters, six grandchildren, and two great-grandchildren.

This is his third novel. Others are *Countdown at Shepherd Square* and *The Duchess and The Ancient Oak*. Several of his short stories are featured in *The Century Anthology*, and his most recent book is a collection of short comedy plays, entitled *Doss and Daisy Dingle and Other Daffy Doers*.